ROSE VERDE

THE COWBOYS OF BLUESONG SERIES

SAVING

Amy Jayden

Get Rose Verde starter library FOR FREE
Sign up for my no spam newsletter and get In Plain Sight, Christmas
Wish and A Journey of redemption and lots more exclusive content,
all for free.
Details can be found at the end of Saving Amy Jayden.

Saving Amy Jayden
The Cowboys of BlueSong Series
Book 1
Rose Verde

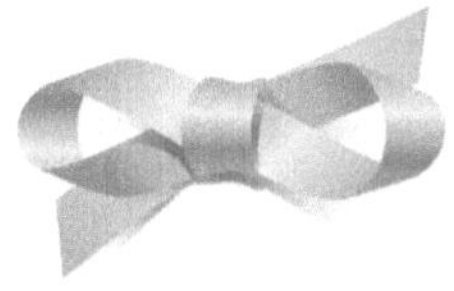

Chapter One

Nevada walked into the kitchen, his Stetson in hand. The ranch housekeeper, Samantha, stood before the giant stove, cooking. The smell of whatever creation she'd come up with this time wafted into Nevada's nostrils, and his stomach rumbled in response.

He smiled. There was never a dull moment with Sam when it came to throwing things together and making a meal, each new recipe something to savor.

"You got grease all over yourself."

"I was trying to fix the truck, but obviously it's not what I think it is. Washed the oil filter, but it's still not working."

"You'll need to call Liam then."

"That's the plan." He washed his hands at the sink, filled a glass with water, and then turned to her. "How's your knee? Still swollen?"

She glanced at the body part in question. "Yes. But the pain killer's helping."

He downed the water. "How about I take you to see the doctor tomorrow?"

"Nah, I'll be fine. And thanks for asking."

"It's not every day you have someone you care about their well-being," he said with a wink.

"You know what?"

"What?" he asked.

"You'd make some young woman happy."

He laughed. "That again?"

"Yeah. And I'll keep saying it until you believe it. The good Lord made it that way, that we share our lives with someone special. And you will recognize the one when you see her."

Nevada wasn't sure about that, but he wasn't about to say so.

"Go freshen up and take that grease smell out of my kitchen." Sam's gruff voice belied her attempt at sternness.

"On my way." He gave her a lopsided smile and a kiss on her cheek.

Sam, widowed and in her early fifties, was like the mother he'd never known. She had helped him fit in quickly, and even though she tried that stern stuff with him, he knew better.

"I'm famished. I'm gonna clean up quickly."

Sam nodded

Pivoting on his heels, he turned to go to his temporary apartment in the loft.

He didn't see his boss Anthony around. Nevada stuck his head around the door. "Is Anthony back yet?"

"Not yet."

"Okay," Nevada responded, peering at the sky through the window and then at his watch. Almost half past ten. Spring didn't yet feel like it in Blue Song. The small town was still down to single digit temps at night. "Let me freshen up then."

He bounded up the stairs, listening to the sound he made as the wood creaked under his weight.

Nevada stood in the shower, hand stretched out to the wall as though to brace himself, his eyes closed. Preparation for the calving season was always swamped with this measure of fatigue, yet it all made him feel alive.

He was doing what he loved and always wanted to do. What he'd lost once—not something he cared to remember—but had the opportunity to do again.

The water cascaded down his body, easing his muscles. They had issues to deal with, uppermost was the expanse of fence that needed repair. But every day as it ended, Nevada was glad he came to Water Hole Ranch.

The weather didn't bother him as long as he had a job to do. It was better than his days of despair. Nevada ran a hand backwards over his hair and down his face, then he turned off the tap and stepped out.

Thirty minutes later, he walked down the stairs and straight into the kitchen. Samantha had the table laid out.

Taking the stool at the kitchen island, Nevada bowed his head in prayer. He took his fork. "Thank you, Sam."

She huffed at him and sat opposite.

Nevada checked his watch. It was now after eleven. "Anthony's still not back?"

"No, not yet," Sam answered.

"That's unusual. What's he doing out so late anyway?" His boss was always in the house reading a book in his recliner before the sun went down.

"He was out fixing that fence on the north while the guys were working on repairing the one on the east. Didn't wanna bother you guys."

"He should've bothered us. That's a job for three men." Nevada checked his watch again. "It's past eleven. He should've returned by now. I better go check with the men."

"He probably just got sidetracked." Sam turned to him. "You know how he gets. Doesn't like to leave things undone."

"Still, he should ask for help." Forgoing his dinner for a bit, Nevada headed out the door. "I'll go find him."

"Thank you, Nevada. I'll keep your dinner warm," Sam called.

Nevada grabbed a jacket on his way out. It was still too cold for spring. Not knowing what to expect, he went with his instinct to drive the truck. He followed the shortest route to the bunkhouse.

"Angel?" Cutting the engine, Nevada climbed down from the truck.

No one seemed to have heard him. Bubbly laughter came from inside the log house. A movement beyond the ranch illumination caught his attention.

"Angel?" he called louder this time; his eyes focused on the movement in the distance.

He could make out the dark image of a horse. He sighed in relief. The horse emerged into the full light, and his respite vanished. No rider. Angel and the others had heard him and trooped out.

"Boss, you called?" Angel asked.

"That's Dark Knight," Nevada said, his heart slamming. "Anthony isn't back yet, and now his horse comes home without him. Get your horses. Angel, come with me. We'll go in the direction the horse came from. The rest of you spread out and search wide. If you find anything, give me a call. Now go! Noah, check on that horse and make sure it's okay."

He didn't wait for a response. Nevada jumped back into the truck. The neighing of horses filled the night as they cantered away. Angel climbed in beside him.

Lord please. Nevada prayed.

He drove the truck north to where Sam had suggested Anthony was last known to be. They had gone beyond the illumination of the ranch light. Where was Anthony? Could his horse have thrown him? Not likely.

Thirty minutes into the search and Nevada had yet to receive any call to indicate any of the search parties had found him. Nevada brought the truck to a place overlooking the ravine at the edge of the ranch.

He left the lights on and climbed down from the truck. "Walk down the other way, I'll cover this side," he said, his hand pointing southward. "Please, watch your step."

Lord, please, was all he could think as he bobbed his flashlight up and down and listened for sound. Minutes and then... He heard a groan, somewhat faint.

Taking careful steps, he walked in the direction of the sound, his ear attentive. A few feet away, he heard the groan again. He quickened his pace and came upon Anthony. He lay further down the slope against a tree root uprooted by erosion. Whipping out his phone from his pocket, he dialed 9-1-1.

"9-1-1, what's your emergency?"

Nevada gave rapid-fire information about the situation.

"Can you please stay on the line? I'm dispatching someone to your location. They should be there in ten minutes."

"He doesn't have the luxury of—"

"I understand that but, that's the closest service to the ranch."

"Okay, please hurry."

"Sure. Stay on the line, all right?"

"Yes." Taking one careful step after another, Nevada reached Anthony. He stooped, using his flashlight to assess Anthony and the area. The tangy smell of blood tickled Nevada's nostrils and he gagged. Anthony's right leg was at a strange angle. Not good. "Boss!"

Anthony Jayden grimaced faintly. His shirt was torn across his stomach. A quick check revealed a gash, a broken stick poking out of it. Nevada's heart sank.

Shrugging out of his jacket, Nevada draped it around him, careful not to jar him. He wasn't a doctor, but from the measure of blood on the ground, Anthony would be lucky to survive.

Anthony gestured weakly, like he was trying to say something, but Nevada could see the effort it cost him.

"Angel!" Nevada hollered into the night. "Over here!" Then he crouched down beside his boss. "Don't try to say anything," he told the man that had come to mean so much to him in the last five years.

Footsteps sounded behind them and then Angel came over and squatted beside Nevada. "How long has he been this way?"

Angel said, "Hard to tell."

Nevada shone the torch on the face of his wristwatch. Barely three minutes. He hated being helpless, knowing that time was ticking for Anthony. Those three minutes didn't begin to compare with long winter nights hiding somewhere in the subway to avoid being caught. "You'll be fine," he whispered, hoping he was right.

"Try to keep him warm." The operator's voice penetrated Nevada's mind. "The air ambulance will be there in a moment."

"Okay."

By the time the chump of the helicopter reached his ears, Nevada was covered in a fine sheen of sweat despite the cold.

The chopper's light flooded the area as it came to land a short distance from them and Nevada had to shield his eyes from the blinding light. He waited until two paramedics reached them before he straightened. A police cruiser pulled up next.

Raking a hand through his hair, he willed his boss to move, groan, anything to say he was hanging in there. Nothing.

"Hansen," the older of the two paramedics introduced himself, talking above the whipping rotor sound. "You have any idea what happened here?"

"No." Nevada stepped away and wiped his brow. One of the police officers approached Angel and was asking him questions. Nevada was thankful they weren't talking to him. His thoughts were for Anthony.

Hansen slipped a neck collar on Anthony and within minutes, they had his leg immobilized, rolls of bandage applied around his torso, the stick still in place.

The younger man tied a cuff around Anthony's arm. They rattled some medical jargon. The phrase "slipped into unconsciousness" jumped out to Nevada. Not what he wanted to hear.

They worked deftly for a few minutes.

"We need to get him up, and then we can put an intravenous line in place."

"Okay. But, how is he?"

"Barely stable. He's lost a lot of blood."

Nevada glanced at Angel. The same fear Nevada was sure reflected in his eyes shone in Angel's.

Seconds later, they lifted Anthony and walked gently but quickly out of the ravine.

Nevada glanced briefly at the policemen cordoning off the area. He rubbed the back of his neck, turning to the paramedics. "Can I come with him?"

"You can come behind us. We'll set up the lines en-route."

Nevada snatched a glance at his boss and willed him to hang in there.

Angel was already calling Daniel to inform him, but they must've heard the air ambulance, because four of them showed up as the ambulance pulled up into the air.

"Daniel, get to the ranch house, tell Sam there's been an accident. We're heading out to the hospital," Nevada instructed.

"Sure."

Nevada climbed into the truck, Angel following suit. Nevada slipped the key into the ignition and missed.

"Are you sure you can drive?"

"Yes." He wiped a shaky hand on his jeans and tried again. The engine roared to life, and he pulled out.

Fifteen minutes later, he drove into the parking lot of the hospital and brought the truck to a halt. Leaving the door open, he ran for the reception area. The nurse informed him that Anthony was already in the ER.

Everything seemed to be moving at dizzying speed. Another nurse came towards them. "Are you here for the patient that was just brought in?"

"Yes."

"We need someone to sign the papers. Are you his son?"

"No, I'm his foreman. Can I sign on his behalf?"

"Does he not have any family?"

"His daughter lives in LA."

"Wife?"

"Passed, a couple of years ago."

"All right, come along."

Chapter Two

Amy Jayden slipped off her six-inch stilettos, her feet sighing in relief. The clock chimed twelve as she padded across the polished wooden floor of her condo. Her friend and roommate, Mel, followed behind stepping out of her loafers.

"Eric definitely pulled out all stops for this party. He may still be nursing hopes that you'll go out with him." Mel's brown eyes that matched her honey colored tresses danced with amusement.

Amy rolled her eyes. "He was hoping I'd hang out with him longer. As if midnight wasn't ungodly enough. He's dreaming."

"Don't think so." Mel gave an exaggerated sigh. "I was afraid he'd put you in the hospital out there with you dancing in those insensible shoes of yours."

Flipping on the light, Amy said, "You know me. Anything less feels like I'm not wearing shoes."

Mel laughed, and Amy joined in.

"I can see you still wearing those things fifty years down the road."

Mel walked on tiptoe like someone teetering close to a precipice. The dramatic depiction only made Amy laugh harder.

They both dumped their bags on the dresser. Mel dropped onto the bed. "If anyone deserves to be manager, it's you, my friend and I'm proud of you."

"Thanks. It's all I've lived for."

"Mm-hmm. But it's going to mean more work, no life."

"You mind explaining what you mean, mate?" Amy said in a fake British accent.

It was her friend's turn to roll her eyes. "You've worked so hard all your life, not even a boyfriend to call your own. Now you've become manager, I fear for you my dear."

"I don't have time for love. I've got all I ever wanted in life."

"I know that's what you say, but it must get lonely without someone to share your life with."

"Nope. Not really."

"Okay then." She crinkled her nose. "Well, I should call Jay. He's still mad that I canceled our dinner for your party."

Amy stepped into the bathroom. "I'll bribe him. Besides, you should tell him we knew each other before you met him." She winked. Mel was already dialing. "I'm going to brush my teeth."

"Come and talk to him," Mel said.

"He's not my boyfriend. He's yours."

"You could get one." Mel stopped abruptly, then she laughed at something Jay said. "It's Amy. She needs a boyfriend." Mel gave her a sheepish grin.

Amy closed the bathroom door. Something pinged in the region of her chest. She wasn't jealous, right? No way, no how. Love made people vulnerable.

Something she never wanted to be.

· · ❧ · ·

"COFFEE." ANGEL PLUNKED into the metal seat in the waiting room. His sandy blond hair looked like he'd plowed his hands through it over and over.

Nevada was sure his hair didn't look any better.

At three am, the hospital was quiet, amplifying the beeping machines that seemed to strum his nerves like guitar strings. He hated the clash of cloying smells he couldn't decipher. "Thanks."

His tummy rumbled. He'd skipped dinner. Nevada took the steaming Styrofoam cup from Angel. He sat up straighter. "You need to go home and rest."

"I'm okay. Besides, I couldn't possibly leave you alone here."

"Don't worry about me. The doctor told me it's going to be an extensive surgery. We've been here for hours and haven't heard anything. There's no point in both of us keeping vigil. Besides there's a lot of work to be done, I'll want you to take charge at the ranch while I'm here."

"Okay, boss." Angel had always playfully called him that.

"Take the truck and make sure to see Sam before heading to the bunkhouse."

"Will do." Angel reached out and squeezed Nevada on the shoulder and then walked out. Nevada sipped his coffee. *God please let Anthony live.*

This man had given him hope, given him the closest thing he'd had to stability.

The man had treated Nevada like a son. If he died, it would be a huge loss, not only to Nevada but their small town. Anthony served selflessly. On the other hand, Nevada's whole dream to buy his own spread would blow up in his face like a puff of smoke.

He'd never met Amy, Anthony's daughter, but from all that he had heard, she wouldn't hesitate to sell the ranch off in a blink of an eye. In the last five years, she hadn't visited the ranch once. He sipped his coffee. *Lord You know what's best and at Your feet I find my rest.*

He downed his coffee, leaned his head back and closed his eyes, fatigue sneaking up on him. Nevada felt a small shake on his shoulder, and he woke up. He squinted trying to bring the man who stood before him in green scrubs and coat into focus. When had he dozed off?

"Sorry I woke you."

Nevada covered a yawn and looked at his watch. *Four am.* Days of making night rounds were taking their toll.

"We just came out of surgery. I'd like to see you in my office."

"Okay, sir. How is he doing?"

The surgeon didn't answer immediately, and bile rose in Nevada's throat. They walked down a corridor and then turned the corner. The doctor opened the door to his office and waved Nevada to a seat.

His belly churned. Shaking himself mentally, he focused on the doctor.

"What happened?"

"I don't really know." Nevada filled the doctor in on all he saw.

"Whatever it was, it was a huge fall. He had major damage to some organs and we removed his spleen. For now, he's in intensive care."

Dr. Clark picked up a pen, dropped it in a holder, and finally made eye contact. "I'll be frank with you. It's not good. The next forty-eight hours will be crucial to his survival. I've placed him into a drug-induced coma to give his body a better chance to heal, we'll have to wait and see. If he doesn't get an infection, which is a major concern, then he'll have a better chance."

Nevada tried to process what he was hearing. His heart beat so fast he feared he'd pass out. *Please God.*

"I suggest you get in touch with his daughter. Have her see me as soon as possible."

"Will do, but, please sir, do all you can for him."

"We'll do our best, but there's no guarantee how things will play out. We'll just have to wait and see."

"Thank you very much." They shook hands and Nevada walked out of the office into the uncertainty that stared him in the face.

• • ∽ᗉᔕ • •

AMY SIPPED AT HER COFFEE and stared at the city skyline through the glass window. She inhaled the aroma and sighed in appreciation.

The toaster spat out her bread. Amy put them on a small plate and made a couple for Mel.

The click-clack of heels echoed down the hall, and a moment later, Mel appeared in the kitchen. Setting her tiny purse that matched hot pink sandals, and her Bible, on the table, she said, "You really should consider coming, just once."

They'd been best friends for years, roommates for three months. Mel made it a point to ask Amy to church every Sunday.

"For the millionth time, Mel," Amy said rolling her eyes, "I'm fine. I don't need anyone."

"It's God we're talking about here."

Amy shrugged. "Breakfast is ready."

Mel shook her head, grabbed her toast and coffee. She added cream and sugar. "Why?" she asked for the first time.

"Maybe, I'm just not ready yet."

Mel opened her mouth, then shut it and started eating. Her look of pity ate at Amy. She'd turned her back on God long ago. He'd definitely not want anything to do with her now.

"You know," Mel started.

Amy's phone rang saving her from whatever it was Mel wanted to say. Every time Mel asked, Amy felt guilty, yet, she couldn't bring herself to go. "Amy Jayden speaking, how may I help you?"

Only silence could be heard on the line and Amy thought the call had been terminated.

Pulling the phone away from her ear, she looked at the screen. The seconds were counting. She placed it back to her ear. "Hello? Is someone there?"

"This is Nevada Logan. I'm the foreman for the Water Hole Ranch. It's about your father."

"What about him?" Something was wrong. The only reason for the foreman of the ranch to call was ... she stared out the window.

"There was an... accident on the ranch. He's in the hospital."

"When did this happen?" Her voice caught, her throat suddenly dry. She set her mug down nearly missing the table.

"Last night."

Amy covered her face with one hand and inhaled deeply. "How bad is it?"

"He's hanging in there. Barely. The doctor thinks the next couple of days are crucial as to whether he'll make it or not."

Amy's belly churned and she feared she'd throw up. It would be difficult to get time away, especially after her promotion. But this was her father. "What has been done for him so far?"

"He's had surgery but the doctors are worried about infection. Your father has extensive injuries and well, because it took so long for us to find him, he lost a lot of blood."

"I'll arrange to be there as soon as I can."

"How soon will that be?"

"As soon as I can," she repeated.

"Did you hear what I just said, Ms. Jayden? Your father may not make it."

Who did this guy think he was? She said she would get there as soon as she could. Did he expect she would just leave her job without giving some kind of notice? "Don't take that tone with me, Nevada Logan. I'll be there as soon as I can arrange it. Let the doctors do their best and I'll be there as soon as I can."

There was a slight pause. She waited.

Silence.

"See you then," she said.

"Sure." He said and clicked off.

Amy leaned against the chair's head rest. She breathed through her mouth to ease the nausea. Definitely not a way to go back home after five years.

"What happened?"

Realizing her hands were shaking; she dropped her phone on her lap. "My dad."

She got up. Mel came around the table and hugged Amy. She blinked to clear her vision, the years stripping back to her mom's accident. She filled her friend in on what the rude foreman told her.

Amy raked a hand through her hair. "Why?"

"I don't know. We don't always have all the answers, Amy."

She stepped away choosing not to give voice to the doubts she'd always had. *Why did God allow such things?*

Mel led Amy to the sofa and sat with her. "You should go so you won't be late."

"I couldn't leave you like this. And don't say no."

Amy nodded, grateful for her friend. "I should call Eric about going home." *Before Nevada thought her callous.* Amy shouldn't care what he thought. He didn't know her.

She wiped clammy palms and dialed her boss.

Mel draped a hand over Amy's shoulder and held her.

Eric's voice came on. "Amy?"

"I'm sorry to bother you," she said quickly.

"Lovely, you know you can call me any time."

Amy chose to ignore the comment. "I need some time away."

"To where?"

"Home. My dad had an accident and I need to get home."

"You have a meeting tomorrow with your team."

"I know that, but this is an emergency." She chose not to add that he may not make it. Her dad had to survive this.

Eric was silent. She hoped his desire to woo her would work to her advantage too.

"How bad is it?"

"I have no idea." Her voice shook and she cleared her throat. "I'll have to get home to find out."

"How long will you be gone? My concern is that you're just starting out."

"I'm aware of that. I could try for a week."

"How about you hold the meeting tomorrow morning? I can get the helicopter to take you home afterward. We can negotiate how long you should take off when you get there and know more."

Amy wondered if she'd be able to sleep that night, much less be coordinated enough to hold a meeting the next morning. But she had to take responsibility for what had been committed into her hands. "All right."

"That's my girl."

The call ended. "I have to hold the meeting with the team tomorrow before I can leave."

"Is he serious?"

Amy leaned against the sofa and closed her eyes. Her strength seemed to have seeped out.

Daddy, why?

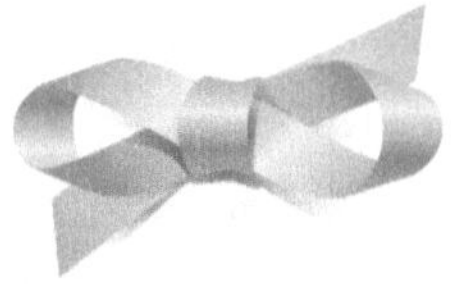

Chapter Three

The gnawing feeling that settled in Nevada's stomach since his talk with Amy wouldn't let up. From the sound of her words, she wasn't going to be easy to deal with. He doubted she cared what happened to her dad. Why would she care anything about the ranch either?

Anthony's life mattered to him so much, Nevada prayed the man survived.

He updated the entry for the calving season in the ranch ledger and headed to the kitchen to eat. He'd had several cups of coffee and his head rang.

The first calf was due in about a week. There was the issue of repairing fences and finishing preparation of the maternity barn for the cows that would calve after the heifers. He didn't have the luxury of sleep just yet.

"Good morning, Sam," Nevada said as he walked into the kitchen. He gave her his customary kiss on the cheek.

"Morning. How did your talk with Amy go?"

"Well, she said she'd be here as soon as she can." He sat at the table.

After the amount of coffee he'd had between when his boss was found and now, he was sure his taste buds were shot, but Sam wouldn't hear of it. She believed people fared better on a full stomach. He couldn't disagree with that.

She set a plate of fried eggs and freshly baked bread before him and gave him that I-don't-think-that-is-all look.

He ignored it and tucked into his meal. It wasn't so bad after all. "This is good, Sam."

"Thank you." She wiped down the table. "You don't think she cares enough."

Though it was a statement, he figured he was required to answer. "Let's just say I'm worried about a number of things and it's coloring everything I see."

She nodded. "Don't be too hard on her. She lost her mother here on the ranch. They were inseparable, those two. That fateful morning a couple of months before you came, Avery fell from a horse and broke her neck. What was worse? It happened right in front of Amy."

Sam took her mug of green tea and sat across from him.

"For days we couldn't get her to eat or talk to anyone. She had a quarrel with Anthony and the next day, she went to stay with a friend. It's been years. Relationships are fragile and we're often not the best caretakers of them. She calls her father on occasions, but the relationship is a strained one and she hasn't shown her face here since."

She took a sip of the tea and looked at Nevada with those piercing motherly eyes. "That one, she's a good kid. Give her time and you'll see it's not what you think."

Sam drank her tea, gave him a smile, and stood, taking her cup to the sink.

"I'll be heading out to the hospital later. Do you want to come with me?" Nevada asked.

"Let me know when you leave. I'll be out back collecting the eggs and milking the cow."

Nevada nodded, Sam's words playing in his mind. A part of him understood Amy's feelings, maybe a little. But the other part thought only a spoiled child would cut off her only surviving parent for whatever reasons she had. He'd give anything to know who his parents were.

Nevada applied mental brakes. They never wanted him. Bringing his mind back to the issue at hand, he sighed. A lot depended on the accuracy of Sam's opinion and he knew she wouldn't lie.

. . ⁓ . .

HOURS LATER, NEVADA brought the truck to a stop in front of the ranch. His eyes were gritty from lack of sleep and too much caffeine.

"I want you to get yourself off to sleep right this minute and not one more word about what you have to do. Do you hear me?" Sam asked.

"Yes, I do." He struggled to keep the grin off his face.

She climbed from the truck and winced. Nevada came down too. Short of hog-tying her and taking her to the hospital to have her knee checked out, he wasn't sure what other approach to take. "Let me help you with this." Nevada reached out to get the plastic grocery bags.

As he made for the front porch, the thump of helicopter blades cut the air. Nevada turned and looked as it flew over the ranch and headed for the helipad a distance from the big old barn. It was the first time a helicopter had landed there since he came to the ranch.

He squinted into the distance. Who could that...?

The high and mighty Amy.

He hadn't expected her to come this quick, at least not thirty-six hours after they had talked.

"Is that Amy?" The joy in Samantha's voice made Nevada curious. Sam stood beside him on the porch, her face wreathed in a big smile.

Not wanting to stand there while Amy came down, he made his way into the kitchen to drop his burden. After putting the groceries away, Nevada lingered. The whole thing was ridiculous.

Was he running away? He rolled his eyes. He hadn't even met her yet. If anything happened to Anthony, he'd do his best for the ranch out of respect for her father, but that's where it ended.

Except that it wasn't cut and dried like that. This was not just the place where he felt at home. It was a place he'd finally succeeded at something.

The sound of the helicopter taking off came to his ears.

"You never came to visit me." The good-natured scolding Sam gave Amy reached him and brought him back from his musing. If he didn't go out and get the introductions done with, Sam would take one look at him and read her own meaning to it.

He stepped out of the kitchen, but the two women didn't turn. Apparently, they were too engrossed in their talk to acknowledge his presence.

Nevada took a look at the woman's attire. *You gotta be kidding me.* Stilettos? On a ranch? She probably thought this was an extension of her office.

He leaned against the wall and watched them. In those crazy shoes, she'd be as tall as his six- two. Her fiery red hair was pulled back in a ponytail and fine tendrils brushed her heart shaped face.

Everything about her screamed class.

Nevada brought his thoughts to a screeching halt. He shouldn't be noticing anything about this girl, he chided himself.

Still, they hadn't noticed his presence. Her gaze swept the rolling hills laid bare by winter. What did she think? What did this homecoming feel like for her? His gaze followed hers. Nature, and particularly the green lushness of the terrain in spring, was his way of reaching the essence of God and His creation.

She gave Sam a hug. "I'm so sorry," Amy said. Her voice sounded strained. "And I'm most sorry I'm coming under this circumstance," she said stepping out of Sam's embrace.

Nevada knew the scolding was nothing. Sam was just that way. When she loved you, she pretended sternness. She loved Amy obviously and the girl could never do anything wrong in Sam's eyes.

Sam was assessing Amy like a mother hen. They were yet to look in his direction. He cleared his throat and they turned simultaneously.

"Nevada! Come say hi to my dear girl."

He met them halfway, wondering what the big idea was. He reached out his hand and Amy took it.

"Nevada Logan, pleased to meet you." He nearly choked on the words.

"Amy Jayden." Her smile didn't reach her green eyes.

Nevada realized his assessment about her height was correct. Belatedly, he released her hand.

Sam clapped excitedly. "Let's get in and you can freshen up."

All thoughts of sleep fled from Nevada's mind. As soon as it was polite enough, he made his excuses and retreated to the den. Sam didn't remember her command that he should get some rest. Plunking down in the leather sofa that graced the corner of the den, he closed his eyes and let a soft sigh swoosh from his mouth.

Amy was beautiful, and her eyes were the greenest he'd ever seen this side of Blue Song. She favored her father but for her mother's fiery red hair. Nevada gazed at the picture on the mantle. The woman stood beside a Chestnut and a small girl, obviously Amy, squatted in front of the horse. Several other pictures graced the walls. Some pictures of Amy on ponies and a couple others of her on horses. He'd seen the pictures many times before but was only now putting the name to the face.

This wasn't the time to start dreaming. He made notes in his book of what to pick up for the ranch in the next couple of days. Once done, he closed it and then picked up his phone and dialed Angel. His voice came on the phone on the second ring. "Hey, buddy, how's the fence coming on?" Nevada asked.

"Good. Thought you said you were coming."

"Yeah," Nevada said, rubbing his eyes. He stayed away from coffee today so that his head wouldn't fall off. Stretching himself out on the sofa, he let his booted feet hang over the edge. "Sam insists I stay put today. She'll have my hide if I do otherwise."

Angel chuckled. "I bet that'll do you some good. See you later then. Meanwhile, the police guy came. He thinks what happened to Anthony was an accident. Nothing to indicate foul play."

"I guess we'll never know what happened."

"That's what I thought, too."

Nevada heaved a sigh. "Okay. See ya." He'd hoped the police would find something to help them understand why Anthony lay critically ill in the hospital.

He dropped the phone beside him and closed his eyes. Maybe he needed some rest after all. Placing a hand over his eyes he sighed deeply.

God please let Anthony live.

Chapter Four

The remodeled kitchen with new marble countertop and polished brown cabinets were another stark reminder of how long she'd been away. What was worse? It took an accident to get her home. Her throat closed up.

Amy filled a cup with cool water from the tap, sipped some and then turned to face Sam. The woman had aged gracefully in the last five years.

When she stood beside Sam's small frame, she became very aware of her own height. Taller than most females her age when she was growing up, she had earned the nickname Willowy. But standing next to Nevada today had made her feel like she had met her— Turning her mind from that train of thought which went nowhere, she focused.

"I see there's a new addition on the loft."

"Oh that? Your dad added it, but Nevada lives up there. Temporarily." Sam bustled about the kitchen throwing together a sandwich for Amy. "Dinner is still a couple of hours away."

"Thanks." Amy accepted the plate from Sam.

They both walked out to the living room and Amy took her favorite spot in front of the fireplace. The warmth wrapped around her like soft cotton. She'd forgotten what the cold felt like here. "Why is he living up there? Dad didn't let any other foreman live here at the ranch house. Why him?"

"Your father expanded the business last year, meaning more calves this year. He took in a couple more hands and let Nevada use the room temporarily until the new bunkhouse is complete. Besides, Nevada is not like the others. He's as trustworthy as they come, and the ranch has made good progress since he came. If anyone deserved that kind of consideration, it's him. He takes on the work at the ranch as though it's his own and fulfills the tasks like clockwork. Since he found your father, he hasn't had a wink of sleep." There was an unmistakable admiration in Sam's voice. No matter what her impression was about him after their phone conversation, she knew she should thank him and maybe even apologize for her sharpness.

Her mind took inventory of the guy against everything she told herself. At least six-feet-two, with piercing hazel eyes, a strong dimpled chin and jet-black hair that brushed his nape. He was a sight.

Taking a swig of her cold fruit juice, she proceeded to eat her sandwich. She wasn't interested in him or anyone else for that matter. She wanted no ties. Her only plan was to take care of her father and be out of there as soon as she could. "How's Dad?"

"Hanging in there."

Amy saw the quick tears in Sam's eyes and her appetite fled. She reached out and dropped her sandwich onto the plate. She felt callous. No matter what problems stood between her and her dad, he should have been her first concern. Guilt rode roughshod over her heart. "Is he that bad?"

"I'm afraid so."

"Then I better get to the hospital." Amy stood up and leaned down to kiss the woman who had taken care of her father while she had gone off doing her own thing. "Thank you for taking care of him and everything around here. I'll go see him now."

Sam shooed her away, picking up the plate and cup as she stood too.

"You might want to ask Nevada to take you. The second truck is not running. I saw him heading in the direction of the den."

"Uh, you think he'll mind? I wouldn't want to bother him."

"No, he won't."

"All right. I'll change and be down." Within minutes, she returned. "I should be back in time for dinner."

"All right, dear. Run along."

Amy walked towards the den. Was asking Nevada to take her a good idea?

. . ❧ . .

"NEVADA?"

Foggy, he came to with a start. When he saw Amy, he groaned inwardly and checked his watch. He'd been asleep for an hour.

What a fine foreman he made, sleeping when he should be out there working. He swung his feet down and got up. Did his head feel clearer? No. He needed more than an hour.

"Sorry. I didn't realize you were sleeping. It is the middle of the day."

Did he hear the accusation in her voice? His defense rose. "Contrary to what you think, I don't sleep away the day."

"Let your hackles down. I wasn't accusing you. I want to go see my dad and wondered if you could take me."

Nevada took in the woman who stood before him, tall and slim. Her fiery red hair flowed down her back, her face devoid of makeup. He kept his defenses up as his shield.

He had to keep his head on his shoulders.

Was Brooke's betrayal not sufficient reason to stay away from females? Besides, her class was way above his league. Clamping down on his mental calisthenics he said, "Give me a few and I'll be ready."

Minutes later, he pulled the truck door open for her and waited for her to climb in. He swung the door closed and pulled out.

The silence in the truck was oppressive. Not that he had strength for chit chatting.

"Are you mad about something?"

"People don't get mad, dogs do." Nevada had to keep from rolling his eyes.

If that was her idea of making conversation, she definitely lacked social skills.

Sam's words came to mind. Was he still letting his impression of her affect his reaction or did he fear she'd judge him as lazy?

"Thanks for helping my father."

He spared her a glance briefly. She sounded sincere. "I'd do that for him any day."

Not what he should say, but she definitely was rubbing him sore. He needed some coffee.

"Look, if it's because I caught you sleeping in the den that's got you in this mood, I didn't mean to come out sounding that way. Sam told me you haven't been sleeping." She clamped her mouth shut. "Forget it."

He was probably rubbing her the wrong way too. He sensed her patience with him wearing thin. Patience was not his best suit, either. They'd make a great pair while she was here.

Amy huffed and fell silent.

Just as well.

He soon turned the truck into the parking lot and cut the engine.

"Thank you," she said again.

"You're welcome." When she would've exited the truck, he said, "You don't have to thank me. What I did for your father, I'd do for mine if I had one. It's no big deal. Besides I'm just a ranch hand and he's my employer."

Amy's face flushed red.

What had he said wrong this time?

Easing from the truck she closed the door not meeting his eyes. "I won't be long."

"Take your time, I'll be here."

Nevada doubted she heard that and he wanted to kick himself. What was wrong with him? He was better at dealing with his anger. At least he thought so, until Brooke betrayal.

That was the problem. When he woke up and saw Amy, he thought he'd been dreaming.

Except that Brooke was shorter and her red hair a couple of shades lighter. That was what triggered his defense.

Leaning his head on the back rest, he closed his eyes.

Father, forgive my anger. I'd have thought I was over this after all these years. What's with me and redheads anyway? To think I just met Amy and I'm not sure of the things that war within me. Correct me, oh Lord, but in Your justice not in Your anger lest You bring me to nothing.

Feeling calmer he got out of the truck, locked the doors, and went to find Amy. It wouldn't do to antagonize her. After all, she didn't do anything against him.

Knocking briefly, he opened the door. Amy sat next to her father, with her head in her hands, telling Nevada that the danger her father was in was becoming apparent to her.

Two days prior, the doctors released Anthony from his induced coma and still he hadn't woken. The doctors didn't seem to hold out much hope. Nevada stepped quietly into the room.

The machine beeped. Anthony's chest rose and fell.

He should leave, but something held him back, he couldn't say what. Nevada squatted beside her, but stayed silent, offering his presence.

He had prayed more than ever in his life since he found his boss. Did God hear all he'd been saying? *Lord please show me You do and let him live.*

Bargaining with God didn't show faith. Did it?

Chapter Five

Amy slipped her phone into her pocket. "Eric says I can take my two weeks' vacation. At least I can be here with Dad."

"That's good," Sam said.

Amy started washing the dishes. Sam was uncharacteristically quiet. What was going on in her mind?

"Did you two have a fight?"

"What do you mean fight?" Amy hedged. She wasn't sure what to make of Nevada. He'd stayed with her like he was offering his...presence, but he'd turned moody on the drive back and at dinner.

Sam clucked. "Don't you think I know you enough to be able to decipher when something is wrong? Amy, I've taken care of you since you were a baby."

There was no getting away. Amy placed the dish she had been drying on the dish rack.

"The tension at the table was so palpable you could cut it with a knife..."

"Dad was not looking well and the doctor told me he developed a fever last night." Amy dropped the towel and her pretense along with it. At that moment, she didn't dare hold another plate or risk it falling and breaking.

She blinked a number of times to clear her vision. Sam wiped her hands on her apron and took Amy in her arms.

"Come on, baby. Where is your faith? God is in control and He knows what's best, okay?"

Amy wasn't sure about God being in control, but she nodded and pushed away, tucking strands of hair behind her ears. After several deep breaths, Amy felt she had calmed a bit and went back to finishing her chore.

"It had nothing to do with the strain between you and Nevada, right?" Sam asked after a moment.

"No."

"No?"

Amy glanced at Sam and gave a small shrug. "He seemed to be angry for some reason. I guess something I said ticked him off." She met Sam's gaze. "Don't look at me like that."

"Like what?"

"Like what-have-you-gone-and-said-this-time kind of look. I know I can be impatient and I'm working on it, but I don't think I said anything that should warrant his anger." Her face threatened to flame at the memory of his outburst. "Maybe he feels threatened by the fact I'm his boss's daughter. Maybe he's afraid he'll have to answer to me…"

Sam placed a gentle hand on Amy's shoulder. "He's had a rough life, Amy. Maybe he's afraid you'll sell if anything happens to Anthony."

"Well, will you blame me if I do? My mother died here and my father lies there dying because he was injured here." Amy's emotions were confusing. She didn't know what was up with them.

"You wouldn't blame him either. In the last five years, I've watched him slave away on this land. If anything, he needs to know his future is not being threatened. Something has driven him on all these years. It's just natural that he's wary of you."

Amy calmed. One thing was certain. She wouldn't keep the ranch for any reason. The bad memories had overridden the good.

"I'm sure you'll sort your differences out, my dear."

Amy rolled her eyes.

"Don't you dare roll those eyes at me, Amy Jayden."

She laughed at the look on Sam's face, the tension from earlier lifting.

"I'm sure Nevada won't have anything to do with me if he can help it. He behaves like I'm an enemy that he can't touch with the end of a stick."

"Amy Jayden! You've only met this guy how many hours ago?" It was Sam's turn to roll her eyes. "Maybe you have a bad case of love at first sight."

"Oh, come on, you are a terrible tease. I'm a city girl, not someone to live on a ranch," she said with finality.

"I guess we'll have to see about that then."

"There'll be nothing to see."

"You'll say I told you so. I'm getting these old bones to bed. Turn off the lights before you head to bed."

"Will do."

Amy stayed in the kitchen sipping tea long after Sam went to bed. It was a mistake staying away so long. She had not seen her father in five years. The few times they talked were painfully short because they had nothing to say to each other. And now - seeing him with all the tubes and beeping machines...

She had wept knowing she may never speak to him again. *Where is your faith?* Samantha's words echoed in her heart. She wasn't sure of the answer to that. Her anger against her dad because of her mother's death left her in a hurry. "I'm so sorry Dad," she whispered.

Why she had ever blamed her father for her mother's death now eluded her. He hadn't been the one to spook that horse. And he'd been hurt just as much as she was. Now it all seemed so petty. She worried that she might not get a chance to apologize for her behavior.

The thud of boots on the porch snapped her from her reverie and she whipped her head around to Nevada, only a couple feet away, knocking off dirt from his boots. Her senses quickened.

"I went to check out the animals. They should be calving in a couple days."

He sounded awkward and she wondered if he was embarrassed about seeing her alone. *He fulfills his duties like clockwork,* Samantha had said.

Amy nodded. He did the same, walked to the sink, and washed his hands. He filled a cup with water and drank it in gulps and then mumbled good night.

She listened to the sound of his feet as he bounded up the stairs to his apartment.

If her father died, nothing would keep her at the ranch and she would hurt Nevada in the process, but she couldn't help that. The land had taken so much from her and she wouldn't retain it.

It was as good as that.

. . ❦ . .

NEVADA TUGGED THE COLLAR of his jacket higher to keep the wind chill out. It was worse on evenings like this. Nobody told the weatherman that the last week in March shouldn't be this cold.

"You didn't say the boss's daughter is back. Heard you took her to see her dad," Angel said.

"Now, where did you hear that?" Gossip was a common thing among the ranch hands and he could only imagine what else Angel had heard. Knowing Angel, Nevada had nothing to worry about.

"Dial went to look for you about something and Sam told him where you went."

Dial wasn't a gossip so he must have a good reason for saying.

"The bank manager sent him to the boss and since he isn't available, I told him you were at the ranch house," Angel said.

It figured. "I didn't know she was coming because she didn't say when she'd come," Nevada responded.

"Who drove her?"

"She flew in on a fancy helicopter." Nevada heard the sarcasm in his own words. "Apparently, she works for a big shot company."

"Man, you sound unhappy about her coming. Didn't you ask her to come quickly?"

Nevada threw the hammer he was using on the fence. It had taken them longer than he thought to fix the fence. After Anthony's accident and the trips to the hospital, he'd had more things to juggle.

Yet, they didn't dare leave the fence that way. What with the calves that would arrive soon. Frustration built in him as he walked towards his friend.

"She's here to see her dad, nothing to be upset about." He didn't say that seeing her cry yesterday had stirred something in him. If he wasn't careful, it would chip away at his defenses. Nevada didn't plan on getting rejected again.

"You think if anything happens to Anthony, she's likely to keep the ranch going?"

"I doubt it." He remembered her stilettos the day she came. "She's likely to dispose of it in as much time as it takes to blink. Look, don't get me wrong. I love Anthony and I respect him and would want him to live for all the right reasons, not just for the ranch. In the times we worked together, he told me she hates the place and Sam thinks so too. And believe me she has reason to." His intensity softened as he thought of the fact that her father's state was good enough reason to hate the place even more.

He leaned on the poles and gazed at the sweeping terrain. In a few weeks, the whole greenery would return along with its beauty. Everything he loved about the land.

"Be anxious for nothing but in everything by prayer and supplication make your request known to God and the peace of God that surpasses all understanding shall guard your heart and mind through Christ Jesus. Philippians 4:6."

Nevada looked at his friend. Times like this his faith didn't even come close to a mustard seed.

"If she sells, you must believe that it's God's time to move on. Who is to say she wouldn't sell to you?"

Nevada snorted good-neighbourliness. "Where would I get the kind of money to buy a place like this? Come on."

They went back to work, each to their own thoughts.

An hour later, they stopped to take a little break.

"The weight of the ranch is on you now. I'm praying for you."

"Thanks, but I'm not taking on what I'm not already doing. Everything else stays as it is. I'm sure the boss will be fine."

"He'll be, definitely. But you'll need to make decisions as the days go by."

Nevada didn't like the sound of that, not because he couldn't handle the responsibility, but because of the implication of it. Anthony had to get better. Nevada surveyed their handiwork. "We should head back. It's getting hard to see."

He picked up the hammer, removed his utility belt and walked toward the tractor, his friend beside him.

Angel's words stayed with him. *Give me wisdom, Lord.* Technically, he'd take instructions from Amy. He didn't want to cross swords with her if she didn't think his opinion was right.

Hopefully, she'd at least want to talk things over.

Chapter Six

It had been a week since Anthony's accident. Everything on the ranch felt subdued. The usual exuberance was gone, even work didn't ease his mind like it used to.

Nevada vacillated between praying for his boss and despair. Nevada asked God to strengthen his faith to believe the best.

Preferring to err on the side of caution, Nevada began checking the heifers every two hours as they got closer to calving.

From experience he didn't want to miss a chance to provide prompt assistance to cows and heifers having problems.

Providing attention to the newborns too was paramount. Their survival depended on how quickly they were dried and fed, not to mention that some first-time mothers didn't take to mothering easily.

He made his rounds quietly.

Another day or two. Juggling between the hospital and overseeing the ranch wasn't easy. Nevada went to the hospital, not because he had to, but because he wanted to. Anthony had given Nevada hope when he didn't think he had any.

"Are you coming to service?" Angel was standing at the entrance of the maternity barn.

"Yeah, I'm done. I'll just go and wash up."

"All right then, I'll go over and clean up, too."

"See you at the barn." Angel turned to go.

Nevada said, "Um, please can you make sure that the stalls are cleaned up first thing in the morning?"

"Will do."

Nevada watched Angel walk away. But for him, Nevada didn't know where he'd be. Five years ago, he'd been sinking into despair, wondering how he'd survive after losing his job at the Lazy D ranch.

Life on the street had lost its appeal and going back to it wasn't what he wanted for his life. Then someone had invited him to a church BBQ. Angel's dad was the pastor of the church.

Nevada had gone for the food and warmth, but that had marked a new beginning. All he needed was a couple more years and he'd have enough to start a small spread.

With this new turn of events, he wasn't so sure. He and Amy had learned to stay out of each other's way, having only polite conversation when necessary. The fact that he was attracted to her scared him into keeping his distance.

After wiping his hands on a towel, he draped it over a post and headed for the house. He had no business feeling anything for Amy. She was technically his boss.

Besides, what did he have to offer?

. . ~∞~ . .

AMY READ THE RANCH ledgers. Obviously, it was making a profit. She checked her wristwatch. Was Nevada planning to show up at all?

It was as though her thoughts conjured him. He stuck his head around the den's door and stepped in.

"You want to see me?"

"Yes. Have a seat."

He glanced at the ledgers and then took the seat in front of the mahogany desk. He sported a two-day-old beard that enhanced his good looks.

Changing the gears on her thoughts, she flipped the pages. "I see the ranch is making a good profit."

"Yes. We had a little expansion last year with twenty heifers. We should see some more profit by the time we wean in the fall."

"At least, until my father's back, while I'm still around, I'd like to know what's—" her phone rang. She glanced at the screen. "Excuse me, it's my boss."

"I was expecting your report today," Eric said.

Dare she remind him she was still on vacation? "I already did that, an hour ago."

"Good. How's your dad? Are you coming this weekend?"

Amy sighed. "Yes. He isn't conscious yet but we're hoping for the best."

Silence stretched on the other side. She felt Nevada's gaze on her and glanced at him. He looked away. "I'll definitely come. I may need to do some back and forth for a while. Ethan keeps me in the loop of how things are."

"Okay. Understand that things can't completely run without you."

"I get that, sir."

When the call ended, she dropped the phone and sighed.

"Wouldn't it be better if you took a leave?"

She massaged her temple to ease the headache that hovered just beneath. For how long would she be able to stand between the two things that tugged at her?

Leaving while things with her father were still uncertain wasn't something she wanted to do. What if he woke up? "I'm actually on leave, which ends this weekend. I just got a promotion to head a new branch of our company."

"I'm sure he understands you need to be here."

"I doubt he does." Not wanting to give him the impression that her work was more important than her father, she changed the discussion. "Back to what we were discussing, I'd love to know what goes on here."

"Definitely." He rose. "Anything else?"

She sighed again. "Nevada, we need to be able to communicate. I need to know what's on your mind."

"I understand you, Amy, and I don't have any problems with your request."

"You didn't think I may have other things to discuss with you?"

He came back and sat down. "Is there anything else you wanted to discuss?"

"No. But, I want to help. My dad would want that."

"You just need to ask—"

"And you answer in a couple of words." Amy pinched the bridge of her nose. "Never mind. I appreciate all you're doing around here."

"Thanks."

"You can go."

He rose. When he got to the door, he said, "I'm praying for you."

Amy's mouth fell open for brief seconds. Not what she expected to hear. "Uh, thanks."

Nevada stepped out. He was praying for her? Reaching out, she picked up the Bible she'd seen Nevada reading a number of times.

She opened the first page, his name scrawled across the top in the same calligraphy that filled the ledger.

She closed it. She wasn't ready to check God out yet.

Chapter Seven

The sun was setting, and the orange ball spread a kaleidoscope of colors on the horizon. Cold wind blew across the land, bringing in the earthy smell Nevada loved. The blazon orange and indigo of the sunset was always awe inspiring for him.

The small barn doubled as a church. It was filled with little friendly chatter. Nevada walked in and was greeted by Mr. Doyle and his wife. They owned the ranch just south of the Water Hole spread.

Doyle was Anthony's close friend. He was a gifted musician. Quiet and reserved, he was a man you wanted by your side in trouble. Their twin little girls giggled as Nevada chucked them on the chin one after the other. He smiled at them and took his seat behind the family.

Sophie, one of the twins, came to him and he sat the little girl on his lap. Daniel walked in with Dial and Angel. Nevada was grateful for these people he'd come to see as his family. The other ranch hands didn't attend church yet, and he hoped he was a good witness. He'd been talking to them and praying. *Lord if it's time for me to move on, give me an opportunity with Lucas, Noah, and Reese.*

As he made an end of his prayers, Sam walked in with Amy. She wore a pink dress and knee length heeled boots completed her look. The pink accentuated the red of her hair. She was easy on the eyes.

Should he have mentioned the bank loan to her? Maybe, not just yet. At least, not until he talked to the manager and knew what to do.

Sam introduced her to the other family and they took their seats. Sighing deeply, Nevada told himself not to stare. But, how could he not? He felt her presence with every fiber of his being.

Reverend Ken walked into the barn signaling the start of service. They sang from a small hymnal that had been passed around the group. As the song, *ABIDE WITH ME*, was sung, Nevada allowed the words to flow over him. *Where everything else fails and comfort departs, help me know You who holds tomorrow abides with me.*

Reverend Ken led them to pray and then asked a few of them to pray for Anthony. The gesture hit a chord in Nevada. Theirs was a group that reminded him of the days of the apostles when everyone loved the other and cared what happened to them.

"We will be looking at the parable of "The Good Samaritan." Let's turn in our bibles to Luke 10. We'll take our reading from verses 25 to 37."

The reverend read the text and then looked at everyone. "We have a tendency to think in terms of group and feel that people in our own circle are better than others."

He let his gaze roam the faces before him. "God is calling us to a walk with Him where we treat people not because of their positions or affiliations but because we see them as people, creatures of God."

He took off his glasses. "God wants us to see people through His own eyes. We need to embrace a life of good will towards everyone. This is the essential ethos of a cowboy." He said with a small smile. "Do not judge others. That was what the priest and the Alleviate did. When you judge, you can't reach out to people."

Was that what Nevada had been doing to Amy?

"This race we run is like going on a trail ride. Every one of us is familiar with that to varying degrees. It's different from my grandfather's days. But we know the trail is hampered with all sorts of hardships. Be ready to lend a hand irrespective of who the person is. That way, we'll be fulfilling God's mandate. May God help us."

"Amen," everyone chorused. The service soon ended and people walked out in the gathering dusk. Nevada lifted the sleeping girl onto his shoulder. His gaze connected with Amy's. Was it admiration he saw in her lovely green eyes? He gave her a small smile.

Sophie's mom came over. "Thanks so much. You're great with kids, Nevada. My girl sits in one place only when she's with you."

He chuckled. "Maybe we have a great connection."

"You can say that. Have a great night."

When she left, Nevada went through the small group, greeting everyone else. By that time, Amy and Sam were heading out. He caught up with them. "Amy, did you enjoy the service?"

"Yes," Amy said, a little hesitant. "I haven't attended church in a long time."

"Then, we'll just bring you more often," Sam said.

After a little more chit-chat, he said, "Sam, I'm going on my next round. Don't hold dinner for me. I'll eat when I get back."

"Okay, dear."

He doffed his Stetson at them, turned and walked away. But all he wanted to do was talk to Amy, know things about her.

• • ✺ • •

AMY WALKED INTO HER room and pulled off her boots, the only ones that still fit, a little. Her clothes and shoes were not practical for a ranch. She was better off in boots and jeans like everyone else, so she made a mental note to go shopping.

Pulling her hair into a ponytail, she changed into her jeans and t-shirt. The words of the reverend echoed in her mind. Had she not judged Nevada when she first met him? Maybe he judged her, but it didn't make it right if she did too.

Amy walked out to the living room. Sam sat in an old rocking chair knitting. "I'm heading outside for a bit."

"Okay, don't be long, it's dark already."

"I won't."

She walked out into the night, and headed in the direction of the maternity barn. She didn't want to analyze why she was heading there.

Was Nevada still there? He hadn't come to the house, but he could be anywhere. She walked into the first lot. Nevada squatted before a heifer. He was drying a calf. She came to a halt just behind him.

"Isn't it beautiful? Newness of life," he asked, excitement showing in his voice. It was the first time he'd said something without sounding like he was setting the boss-employee boundaries. She rolled her eyes.

How did Nevada know she was behind him anyway? He had yet to look up. Not knowing what to say, she walked fully in and squatted beside him.

"I came here during a calving season—not like I hadn't experienced a whole bunch, but the experience stays the same—awe, appreciation for the new things of life."

He sat on his haunches. "So, that day, like this, we had been checking the lot for nearly a week," he looked at her with a smile that sent her pulse skittering.

So, he knew it was her?

"And this particular night, I was checking the heifers out and right before my eyes a calf was born. At the previous ranch I worked, we celebrated every first birth. I've tried doing that since I came here."

"Why?"

"It was a fresh start for me and I knew I wasn't going to make the same mistakes that got me thrown—" Seeming to catch himself, he rose and took the calf to its mother. His profile to her, he watched the calf teeter on shaky legs, fall a couple of times and finally get its balance and begin to suckle.

The smile on his face was something Amy had never imagined. She remembered him and one of the Doyle kids at the service. There was something about this guy.

She used to love coming around the maternity barn as a kid. Something she now hated. Amy hoped her father made it so Nevada could keep working the ranch. His love for the place was apparent. She could only imagine what would happen if she put the ranch up for sale. He'd be really hurt.

"I'm sorry, I got carried away. Did you want something?" Nevada asked.

Amy saw the flash of hurt in his eyes and then it was gone so swiftly she could imagine it. The set of his jaw told her she hadn't. He'd seen she didn't share his excitement.

She rose. "I was just walking by."

He nodded. "I'll just go check the others." He turned and walked out of the lot. But, as she watched him walk away, she remembered why she came. Anyway, it was too late to rectify the problem. It was like they'd taken a step forward and two steps backward.

She returned to the house.

Amy dropped into the glider and set it into motion. She couldn't appear before Sam just yet. Why did she get so irritable around him? Was she jealous of the fact that her father loved the guy?

There had to be something her father saw in him. It was apparent in the fact that he lived in the loft, albeit temporarily. He ate at their table. The staircase to his apartment ran through the house. He was practically in the house every spare moment he had.

He didn't ask her to stay away. Did he? Why was she taking him to task for something that was no fault of his? Or was she fighting her attraction to him?

No way. She let the swing go and closed her eyes feeling the cold breeze in her hair. She shivered.

"Isn't it getting cold?" Sam asked.

Amy's eyes snapped open. She brought the glider slowly to a stop.

"What's the matter?"

"Uh, nothing," Amy said.

"You don't want to go through that again, do you? You swing that way when something bothers you. Besides, you were so lost in thought you didn't hear the door. Not that it's quiet. Is it...?"

Amy's hand shot in the air. "It's nothing, Sam. I promise." Amy stood. "I'm going to wash up and go to bed." She kissed Sam and walked away.

"When will these children learn to exist together?" Amy heard Sam ask.

Existing together wasn't the issue. Nevada was stirring up things in her she didn't want to confront. And once her dad recovered, she was going back ... to the life she knew.

Chapter Eight

Amy looked out the window to see what was responsible for the early morning excitement. She did a quick headcount of the cowboys, nine of them including Nevada.

How did they deal with the cold all dressed in nothing but long-sleeves? The temperature was still in the single digits, especially in the mornings and nights.

She singled out Nevada in the mix. While the others were talking at the top of their voices, he commented in low tones, chuckling occasionally. What was all the noise about, anyway?

Then she remembered. They were celebrating the new calf. What had he said? *"Newness of life."*

Sam appeared with a tray of cookies.

They practically dragged it from her and before Amy could blink, they had the cookies in their hands. She was surprised at the camaraderie. A small smile tugged at her lips. Maybe there was something nice about life on the ranch that she'd missed after all.

Everyone in the city was prim and precise. There were fun things and places, but not like when people took joy in mundane things. Who would imagine anyone celebrating a calf?

Sam said something, everyone laughed and then she walked back with her tray.

"Work begins and you all get my usual coffee as reward," Sam shouted over her shoulder. "I'll keep it on so you can come get it."

Were there more calves?

Amy entered the kitchen. "I can see you are all excited." She cinched the belt of the robe she had thrown over her night dress.

"Yes, a number of heifers had their calves overnight. Nevada is always excited, insisting it's worth celebrating."

"That's good, but I don't see the big deal."

"You have been away too long. Calving for some is newness, for others it's like a fresh start."

That again.

Sam set the coffee maker on and pulled out a thermos.

"What do you want me to do?"

"Wash these thermoses."

"OK. But, what do you want to do with six thermoses?"

"Coffee. The stuff the cook gives them at the bunkhouse is not as good as mine," Sam said.

"Can't he get the type you buy?"

"It's not about the type as much as it has to do with the way it's prepared. Come on, stop being a wet spot..."

Sam's sudden quietness made Amy look up from her washing task. She took in the narrowed eyes and knew she'd been found out.

"Nevada said one was born yesterday. You knew that though, didn't you?"

"Yes, I did and obviously I don't get what all the excitement is about..."

"And you told Nevada that?"

Amy shrugged. "Not in so many words."

"You should work on hiding your feelings a bit better."

"I'm just not good at pretending."

Even though Sam wasn't angry at her, Amy could have applied some diplomacy. At first, she'd been awed until she saw the excitement fade from his eyes and then she'd thought, what's the big idea?

"Here, your thermoses are ready. I'm going to see Dad."

"Could you pick up a few groceries for me if I give you a list?"

"How will I get them home? The other truck is bad, remember?"

"Nevada can take you. Or if he's busy, ask to use the other truck. He said the mechanic is coming later in the day."

"I don't think I want to ask him again."

"He'll gladly do it." Sam's eyes bore into her and Amy shifted under her gaze. Why was Sam bent on throwing them together?

Amy couldn't remember the last time she had this measure of difficulty relating with someone. "No, he'll do it out of a sense of duty."

"Give him a break and don't roll those eyes."

"I'm not," Amy said laughing. "With all the work going on..."

"He'd have been the one to take me, since I can't drive with my bad knee. The earlier both of you learn to exist together the better you'll be. Now run along."

Nevada walked in just then. He cut his gaze to her and nodded, giving her a cool good morning. Blushing painfully, she returned his greeting.

What was wrong with her? They were both behaving like a married couple.

"I trust your night was good?" he asked, like he really cared.

If he was putting up a front for Sam, he was doing a fab job of it.

"Fine."

He nodded and looked away. Sam busied herself filling the thermoses. What would she think?

"I want to go see my father and then pick up a few things. I was wondering if you could take me... but if you can't, I'll find a way." She hastened to add. She didn't say his name, but he'd know she was addressing him.

Before he opened his mouth, Sam cut in.

"You'll take her Nevada, because she's shopping for me. She can't lug groceries back by herself." Her tone brooked no contradiction.

Sam was meddling. To what intent? They were bound to irritate each other more at this rate. "When will you be ready to go?"

"As soon as Sam draws up her list." Amy didn't meet his gaze.

"Meet me outside when you're set."

She stepped out of sight, but stayed behind the door so she could see them. Bad habit, yeah, she knew that.

He turned and encountered Sam's gaze.

"I know what you think. I'm making an effort and I'll try harder."

"I know you will," Sam said.

He nodded and poured himself coffee. "See you when I get back." He kissed her on the cheek and went out with his cup of coffee. He had given his word, but maybe she was the problem. Maybe she was difficult to get along with.

. . ❧ . .

"I'M SORRY ABOUT YESTERDAY." His eyes left the road briefly to look at her. "I won't make any excuse for myself. I'm not very good at..." He turned his attention back to the road. "I want us to start afresh and at least get along."

"I'm sorry too. I haven't behaved well, either."

Her frankness was refreshing. "So, can we forget that and move on?"

"I guess we can," she said smiling, her cheeks dimpled. Why hadn't he noticed that before? *How would you when you spend all your time keeping your defenses up?*

Amy wasn't Brooke, but he wasn't ready to test the waters. Not with his boss's daughter anyway. Yet, nothing said he couldn't get along with her.

When he cut the engine, he said, "Go on and see your father. I'll see if the doctor's around, then meet you there unless you want to talk to him too."

"No, I'll just go see Dad." She exited the truck and walked in the direction of the hospital entrance while he found a spot to park.

Her scent lingered, soft, alluring, it reminded him of summer. His attraction to Amy was getting stronger. But who wanted a street kid with no roots? Brooke definitely didn't.

I do.

I know You do, Lord. And, I'm grateful for that.

Good. I want you to know that. Be patient. Trust the process, the small voice whispered.

Yes, Lord.

He climbed out of the truck. Was he ready for whatever *the process* meant?

Chapter Nine

The butterflies set off by his lopsided smile quieted some. She was glad they had reached a truce.

If anyone asked her why they didn't seem to get along, she wouldn't know exactly what to say. Assumptions that it was for fear of his future were just that, assumptions. He didn't strike her as a chauvinist, so the idea he didn't want to answer to her didn't come in.

She rounded the corner and stepped up to the nurse at the station. "Good morning. I'm Amy Jayden. I'd like to see my dad Anthony Jayden."

"You know his room number?" The nurse whose name tag read *Lorraine* smiled at Amy.

"I do."

"All right, go on up. I'll be with you shortly. "

Amy thanked her and walked away. Stepping into the clean room moments later, the smell of antiseptic hit her and flooded her with memories of the day her mother had been brought in here.

Amy shook her head, clearing it of the memories. Taking the only seat beside his bed, she held his hand. The gentle rising and falling of her dad's chest reassured her he was still there.

But, for how long?

There was a gentle knock and the nurse walked in. "I'm Lorraine. I want to change some of his gadgets." She went on to explain all that she'd be doing with the wound drains, catheter and feeding tube.

She couldn't be much older than Amy's twenty-six years. Lorraine's manner was respectful. Her likeable persona drew Amy in.

She watched the lady as she deftly changed the tubes on the appliances. When she removed the tube in Dad's nose and proceeded to put another in, Amy broke out in a fine sweat.

She stepped away towards the window and took several calming breaths. The man in the bed didn't resemble the father she once knew. Strong, quiet, and accomplished. How could he be reduced to this helpless person on the bed? Her throat tickled. Amy closed her eyes and bit down hard on her bottom lip.

"All done," Lorraine said.

Amy blinked to clear her vision, and to gain a measure of control. She turned. "Do you think he'll pull through?"

Lorraine was thoughtful for a moment.

"Physical evidence points otherwise." She faced Amy, her ever present smile in place. "But, in medicine, we've learned to never say never. Some patients defy all odds and against every possible explanation they take a turn for the better. We are doing all we can and hoping for the best."

She pressed a lever to change his position and then came to stand beside Amy, placing a hand on her shoulder. "If you have any concerns, you might want to speak with the surgeon." Lorraine held Amy's gaze. "All things are possible with them that believe."

Amy nodded, not sure she could speak past the lump lodged in her throat. Unfortunately, she didn't believe in God. Stopped believing, was more like it. If her father died without waking, she didn't know how she'd live with the guilt.

There was another knock on the door and Lorraine gave her shoulder a gentle squeeze and stepped away as Nevada walked in.

Amy took the seat again. She ran her thumb over the blue veins that stood out on her dad's hand. They looked strong. He didn't appear anything like his fifty years.

Where were all her Christian beliefs when she had blamed her father these five years? "What did the doctor say?"

Nevada's hesitation told her all was not well.

"We should be hopeful, nothing is impossible…"

"That didn't answer my question, did it?" She pinned him with her gaze and dared him to lie to her face.

He gave a small shrug. "He's not very hopeful… but it doesn't mean we can't be." He hastened to add.

She pushed a shaky hand through her hair then placed her father's hand gently on the bed. Amy stood and walked up to Nevada. She folded her hands on her chest and looked at him. Her throat worked for a moment before she made herself speak. Self-deprecation filled her. "My mother wasn't pushed. She knew how to ride well. The horse got spooked and she was thrown. She landed on her head and died en route to the hospital."

Something flashed in his eyes. Compassion?

Letting the tears flow she swallowed and continued. "Maybe if she wasn't upset because she and my father had argued that day, she'd have paid more attention. I left home the day after she was buried and didn't look back until this… What kind of child does that?"

Nevada straightened from where he leaned against the wall. "You were hurting. Don't be hard on yourself."

She felt like a lost child. His words only made her cry harder. Amy covered her face. When he drew her into his arms, it was tentative, like he half expected her to push him away.

Amy clung to the lapels of his coat and wept. He held her, his musky cologne surrounding her. Though it was out of sympathy, it felt good.

She sniffled. "I don't know how I'll be able to live with myself if he dies."

"Don't think that way."

She didn't miss the sadness in his voice. Was it because of her father or the ranch? The ranch's continuance depended on her father's survival. She wouldn't want to stay back on the ranch, wouldn't even know how to start running it.

She stepped out of his embrace, heat suffusing her face. "I'm sorry, I'm never like this."

"Don't worry about it. Let's stay hopeful. Okay?" He produced a clean bandana and handed it to her.

She nodded. Silence stretched out between them, but not the usual tense quietness.

He checked his watch. "Eleven a.m."

They'd been there for almost an hour.

"Are you still up to shopping? Sam will understand if you can't," Nevada said.

"I can't make you come all the way and not do what—"

"It doesn't matter. I'll bring you when you are ready."

"Thanks..." She bit her lip. "I misjudged you..." She broke off and gave him a small smile. "If the other truck gets fixed, I could go alone. If not, can we go tomorrow?"

"Your wish is my command." He swept her a small bow and she worked up a smile.

"I'll stay a bit more. Can you pick me up in the evening, say four pm so that I don't keep you from work?"

"Four it is then." He walked out.

Let everything be alright, she pleaded.

And the thought jolted her.

• • ❧ • •

IT WAS NEARLY MIDNIGHT when Nevada returned to the house. Amy sat in the glider, a duvet around her. "It's cold," he said.

"Yeah, and it's supposed to be spring."

Nevada chuckled. "You can say that again." He slid onto the glider. She'd been quiet all through the drive home from the hospital. He could imagine what was going through her mind and decided to give her space. "You're not sleeping. Are you okay?"

"Who says I'm not fine?" Her tone was quiet, subdued.

He stared at her face in profile for a few seconds. "It helps to talk about whatever is bothering you."

"It doesn't help if the one asking is the one bothering me." She smiled, but he could see her eyes shone with unshod tears.

"Am I disturbing you?"

"Uh, no. I was just joking."

"Amy, you need to rest more."

"What if he wakes up and I'm not there?" Amy swiped her cheek.

The words cut him. She couldn't be there round the clock, like now. But he didn't point that out. He reached out and took her hand, offering his strength where words failed.

"How are you always so sure?"

He looked at her, but she didn't meet his gaze. "About what?"

"Your faith." She shrugged. "What's it like for you?"

Nevada didn't talk about his past. The scripture from 1 Peter 3:15 came to him. *Always be prepared to give an answer to everyone who asks you to give the reason for the hope that you have.*

Was that what God wanted from him?

"You don't have to say anything if you don't want to."

He squeezed her hand and set the glider in motion. "I'm not always so sure about a lot of things. A lot. But, one thing I know is that if God loved me enough to send Christ to die for me, then, He loves me enough to have my back."

He stopped. Was he communicating properly?

He was never good with words. That's the reason he'd always resorted to anger and physical measures when things didn't go his way. He'd nearly knocked out his previous boss's teeth.

Thankfully, the man had not pressed charges against Nevada. Finding himself back on the street at twenty-two had been his wake-up call.

He'd been good at what he did and knew if he got his act together, he'd do well.

There was no way he could have fixed himself, but God did.

Still was working on him.

Amy squeezed his hand bringing him from his reverie.

"I didn't always believe. Growing up as a street kid didn't give you much to believe in. You just survived somehow. And I made a lot of mistakes in the process." He sighed and traced his thumb across her hand.

Amy was the first person he was going in-depth with. Even when he and Brooke dated months before, he hadn't told her much.

He was glad he hadn't, because he obviously wasn't good enough for her, even without her knowing his baggage. "It's a long story. When I met Angel, it was during their church's rally in preparation for a new year's program. His dad's a pastor. I only went because they had a potluck and at least I'd have my stomach filled for that day and a warm place from the cold."

He smiled at her and she reciprocated.

He couldn't figure out yet why he felt comfortable sharing his past with Amy. "At the program, God made me an offer I couldn't refuse. The rest is history."

"Wow." Her voice sounded breathless, stirring something in the region of his heart.

"Faith is a walk, not some sprint or hundred-meter dash. It's not always easy. It's a daily conscious choice. I look to what He did for me, wanting and accepting me when no one did. It was a proposal I couldn't decline."

Amy covered her face with the other hand, sniffling.

"Hey, I didn't tell you to make you cry."

"It's not that." Her voice wobbled.

He tried to take her hand off, but she wouldn't let him. "What is it? You're making me feel bad. I thought you wanted to hear about my hope."

She dropped her hand. Her eyes were red with pain written in their depths. Nevada wanted to kiss her aches away, assure her that all would be well. But they both had baggage they were dealing with.

He wasn't good enough for her. All he could do was pray for her, hope that she found her way out of the guilt that held her.

"I'm sorry—"

"Come here." He held her, not knowing what plagued her.

God, I sure have messed things up.

No, son. She's going through a process. Trust me on this.

Process again. He sighed. You sure have a lot of those going on, Lord. But, please make it easy on Amy, especially with her father.

I wound and I bind.

Nevada didn't like the sound of that. But he'd learned that "all things work together for good" didn't mean all those things would be good things. He hadn't fully realized the good in all he'd gone through in the past, but the fact that God was working on his anger issues was one.

If his story tonight helped Amy, that was another good.

He hoped.

Chapter Ten

Nevada needed to stop thinking of himself. If Amy did sell the ranch, she had every reason and right to. The scene from the day before played on his mind all last night, kept his sleep at bay. Somehow, she'd woken up a protective instinct in him like he hadn't felt for anyone.

When he'd held her at the hospital, he hadn't been thinking anything of it. In his wildest imagination, he'd never thought she'd let him hold her. From the way she blushed, she must have been embarrassed.

He smiled to himself.

He hadn't met someone who blushed over everything. And then he'd held her again last night and it felt natural. He wanted her to be happy.

Nevada walked into the maternity barn. The ones that had calved had already been moved to another part of the ranch. No new calves tonight. He made his way to check the new mothers and their babies.

The novelty of the first week was ending with sore muscles for everyone at the end of each day. The maternity barn was closer to the bunkhouse, but with other work going on, everyone needed as much rest as they could get, hence the night checks fell to him and Angel.

With a heifer in the second stage, it was better to stick around. He walked out into the night and sat on the boulder beside the maternity barn. It had drizzled earlier. Unfortunately, it had turned to hail, making the weather chillier.

He gazed into the night sky, breathing in a lungful of clean air. The peak of the period was hitting them faster than they expected leaving little time for reflection on new life.

He chuckled to himself, remembering how he'd had to break up a near fight between Tagger, the burly Irish man, and Dial, the Spanish agriculture student, over coffee. Black looks abounded in good measure over coffee and they'd already run through Sam's supply.

His thoughts went to Anthony during this time and Nevada's smile slipped.

Anthony hadn't regained consciousness and it'd been over a week, closer to two.

A sigh escaped Nevada.

One thing gave him rest. Anthony was a Christian in every sense of the word. Even though Nevada didn't like the way the man most likely would meet his maker, he had hope of eternity.

Where did that leave Amy? She hardly left her father's side these days. Nevada took her there in the evenings and brought her back in the mornings. Between that and the ranch work, his days were full.

Nevada dropped his head in his hands and let the tranquil atmosphere wash over him.

He glanced at his watch. Half hour since he last checked the animals.

First time mothers sometimes had problems but in the last one week plus, it'd been smooth sailing for them.

He did a quick round and then went to the laboring heifer. She was straining. The calf's head protruded, but only one leg. She'd looked like she was progressing well the first round.

Just in case she was having difficulties, he gathered supplies—soap, buckets, gloves, lubricants, chains, Oxycontin—into the calving stanchion.

"Trouble?" Angel asked, walking in.

"I guess."

Between them, they had the heifer standing, restrained in a head-catch. After scrubbing the perineal area, he did a quick but thorough scrub of his arms. Angel handed him the plastic gloves and helped him squirt an ample amount of sterile lube on.

"Why didn't you come get any of us? It'd make things easier."

"I just saw this. Besides, I figured you all needed your rest for one night." Nevada pushed the calf back in gently as far as he could, then felt for the leg.

He cupped the hoof and maneuvered it. Now, the head rested on the knees and both feet were presenting in the birth canal. He felt over the top of the calf's forehead. Satisfied that there was enough room to allow the calf to be born, he withdrew his hand.

The cow lay down and strained. Nevada grabbed a leg and pulled, then let go when the cow rested.

"That means you haven't gone to bed at all?"

"No," Nevada said shortly.

Angel gave Nevada a look that he chose to ignore. He was only considering them the way he'd want someone to do for him.

The process went on for about half an hour—pull, rest, and pull again. The cow's moo rent the night and the calf slipped free.

By now, Nevada and Angel were both covered in a fine sheen of sweat despite the cold night.

Angel took over with the calf while Nevada assessed the cow.

"It's weak, but thank God it is breathing. I'll need to bottle feed."

"Go ahead. As far as I can see, no tears." Nevada got the cow up.

"You're skillful. I wasn't expecting any problems with the cow or calf."

"Sometimes even the best skills don't pan out."

Angel went to the kitchenette to prepare the bottle. He sat on his haunches and tried getting some milk down the calf's throat.

"I just felt I should check again before I turned in, just in case I didn't wake up on time for another round."

"I always set my alarm, Nevada. You have a lot on your plate to worry about. I could check them."

"I think he's had enough." Nevada applied a tag on the calf and between them they moved it with the new mother to another warm empty clean stall. The cow began to lick the calf immediately.

"Our work is done." Nevada picked up a bucket and walked to the tap to wash.

"How will you do this loan thing? The boss isn't here now to deal with that."

Nevada thought of the lodge on the south side of the ranch. He and Anthony had looked at the possibility of making more money for the ranch if they could provide accommodations and have people vacation there.

"I haven't figured it out yet. Four weeks is short but hopefully, I'll be able to work something out. The poor sales on the steers contributed to the delay."

Nevada had been learning to trust God for everything; he wouldn't let that burden him right now.

"Does Amy know?"

"No. She has her father to worry about."

"You should let her know."

Nevada shook her head. "Considering her feelings for the place, I'm not sure it's a good idea."

"I'll be praying for you."

"Thanks, buddy, for everything."

Nevada shook the water off his hands and faced his friend. Who knew if he'd have this opportunity to say this again? If the ranch got sold, everyone would be considering the next way forward. "If we have to leave here maybe in the intervening weeks, I know one thing is certain, meeting you five years ago- it feels like yesterday, right? It changed my life. Don't know what I'd have done with my bitterness and all that..."

His throat clogged and he found himself in his friend's embrace.

"I know the thoughts that I think towards you," Angel quoted from scripture. "I was just an instrument. God had it planned out before you were born." He released his friend. "God is still in charge no matter what happens."

Nevada nodded.

"I'll be checking in on my parents later today. My mom's a bit under the weather," Angel said.

"My greetings to them."

"Sure. Don't bother coming out again, I'll check them." He clapped Nevada on the back.

"See you around then."

"Yeah."

· · ❦ · ·

"YUCK, ALL THIS DUNG." Amy scrunched up her nose at the copious manure on the front porch. Sam laughed at Amy.

"City girl, this is what you get with the frequent tour for coffee. I'll clean it out as soon as I finish here," Sam said from her place at the kitchen window.

Amy skirted around it and stepped into the kitchen where Samantha's arms were waiting. "How's Anthony?"

"I've just about given up hope. Everything I hear doesn't give me much to hold on to. Lorraine tells me things just to make me feel good but that's it." She stepped out of Sam's embrace, removed her sweater, and draped it over the key hanger, plunking onto the stool at the worktable.

"You look tired," Sam said.

Amy massaged her temples fighting the tears that hung beneath the surface. It made her feel needy and scared. "I guess I am."

"Anthony wouldn't ask this of you, you know that?" Sam pulled out the roast from the oven and set it on the worktable. Removing her mitts, she sat beside Amy taking her hand.

The tears welled and spilled. A mixture of fatigue, guilt and frustration hit Amy in the gut like a battering ram.

"I'm afraid he'll wake up briefly and I won't be there to ask him for forgiveness." She retrieved her hand, took out her handkerchief and wiped her face.

"What's happened has happened. Quit beating yourself up over it, okay?"

"I wish I could."

Footsteps sounded on the stairs. Amy flushed and got up. "I'll go catch some sleep." She turned and almost collided with Nevada's broad chest.

"Whoa," he said, his hand steadying her.

She mumbled her apology and fled. Remembering her sweater, she came back for it. She caught Nevada's gaze. He looked at her in a strange way. Heat burst in her face and she snagged it and hurried away. What would he think about her new penchant for tears? Not the impression she wanted him to have.

Chapter Eleven

Nevada frowned at the warmth that ran down his arms from contact with Amy. "Is she all right?"

"Anthony's not doing well and she's afraid he'll die."

He had enough reasons to think so, but he wasn't about to give his opinion voice. The reality gave him unease in no small measure and he ached for Amy.

He took his seat and Samantha placed a plate of rice and chicken on the table. Bowing his head, he prayed and started to eat. "I guess we all have our individual demons to deal with," he said thinking of what she told him the day they decided to come to a compromise. "I'm going to town to buy some colostrum for the new calves. We've exhausted what I bought earlier. Angel's mum isn't feeling well so he can't pick it up. I'll stop by to see her while in town."

"I hope it isn't something serious."

"I don't know exactly. He isn't so sure either. We'll know more when I get there."

"My regards to them. Meanwhile, come back to the kitchen when you're ready to go. I'll have something packed for them."

Nevada gave her a lopsided smile. "Thank you."

He set his spoon down, his eyes on Sam, wondering about the emotions that seized him. He loved this woman like he would love his own mother. What if they all had to go away?

"What are you thinking that you're looking at me that way?"

Nevada picked up his spoon and turned his gaze to his food. "I'll really miss you when I leave here."

Sam turned to him, hands on her hips and asked. "Who is saying anything about anyone leaving anywhere?"

He looked up, smiling in spite of the pain that twisted his insides like a knife. "Nobody, but I have looked at it from all sides and it's best I get used to the fact that this is not my future."

Thankfully, he had some money put away. He'd do everything to keep off the street here on out.

Hot tears burned his throat. Getting up, he picked at his half-eaten meal. He wasn't an emotional person and couldn't understand what was wrong with him.

He walked to the sink and began to clear the dishes. Thankfully, Sam didn't say anything more. He guessed it was obvious to her what he said was true.

He finished his chore and ended up in the den feeling chafed and raw.

If he didn't make an effort to update the records, he'd soon start having lapses and that didn't bode well for planning. Other years, he'd have everything down pat and buttoned up tight.

Sitting at the desk, he rubbed his eyes as though to push the fatigue out. He updated the number of calves, expenditures for repairs and the construction—all of which Amy had approved with more ease than he expected.

That out of the way, he picked up his Stetson and slapped it on his head. He'd swing by the construction site on his way and see how far it'd come along.

Lord I need Your help so I don't crumble under the weight of this burden.

• • ❧ • •

NEVADA FOLLOWED HIS friend into his parents' room.

"Mom, why didn't you tell me earlier?" Angel asked propping her with pillows to make her comfortable.

"I know what this time of the year means for you. I couldn't add to your burden. I'm fine now. The doctor said I picked up a bug. I guess I'm getting old."

Nevada could see she was making an effort for her son's sake. "I thought I'd come and say hi after Angel told me. How are you doing?"

The woman's brown eyes crinkled. "Seeing both of you now, I feel better."

"That's good to hear."

Angel waved Nevada to the sofa in the tastefully furnished room while Angel sat beside his mom holding her close. "You have a fever. You should've called me. You're more important than work, okay? Promise me you'll tell me if anything is wrong."

Nevada watched the exchange between mother and son. When he used to come to their house, he'd watch Angel with his parents and wonder who his parents were. "What Angel said is correct."

She looked at Nevada and nodded, her brown eyes bore into him with uncanny perception. "You look tired."

"I guess I am."

"Is that my boy?" Rodriguez's voice boomed across the foyer.

Angel smiled. As far as his dad was concerned, Angel was always a boy. "Yes, Dad."

"Welcome, Son," Rodriguez hollered.

"Thanks, Dad. Come see who's here."

The microwave door closed and a soft whir followed.

Minutes later, Pastor Rodriguez showed up with a tray and set it on the table by the bed. The aroma of chicken noodle soup wafted through the room.

Nevada rose.

The man reached out and pumped him on the shoulder. "We miss you around here, son."

"I miss you both too. Calving is gradually winding down. I should be able to come by more often."

Angel's dad nodded. "I got some chicken noodle soup for her. She's hardly held anything down the last few days."

Angel took the soup from him. One look at his dad, he said, "I'm sorry I'm not able to be around much." He spooned some into his mother's mouth.

"No worries, boy. How's Anthony?" Rodriguez directed the question to Nevada.

"Same. The surgeon's concerned about the continued state of unconsciousness. They said something about overwhelming infection, whatever that means."

"I can imagine what work must be like for you all. I could come and help, you know?" Pastor Rodriguez said.

"Maybe when mum is well. Everybody's pitching in and doing their best," Angel said.

"How's Amy?"

Nevada's heart lurched at the mention of her name. He tamped it down willing his racing heart to settle. "She's fine. Busy with her father." It wasn't his place to say that she was doing it out of guilt. Everyone made mistakes, some they can fix, others they couldn't, so they learn to accept and live with it.

Angel settled his mother back in his arms.

"Now that you are here, I better run some errands," Pastor Rodriguez said.

"All right, run along but be quick, so I can return to work."

"Take your time, Angel. I'm going to pick up the supplies and head back to the ranch."

"Thanks, bud."

Pastor Rodriguez kissed his wife on her head and squeezed his son on the shoulder. "I'm sure your mum will be better today since you came. She's eaten more than she has in days."

Nevada didn't miss the twinkle in the man's eyes as Rodriguez looked at his wife of twenty-nine years or the answering smile his wife gave.

From what Angel said, they couldn't have any other children. His mother had told him she had a severe fever after his birth, and the doctor said she'd had an infection in her womb that killed her chance of having more children.

Looking at them, their challenges had not killed the love they shared.

Nevada envied their kind of love, wished for that kind of connection with someone. He thought he'd had it with Brooke.

His thoughts went to Amy, and he pressed the memory away from his mind. She wasn't his kind, and as painful as it was, he had to face the truth, so he didn't get hurt.

When the pastor left, Nevada followed. A thought occurred to him. "Pastor Rodriguez, mind if I ask you a question."

"What is it, son?"

He didn't know much about Pastor Rodriguez, but he did know he wasn't yet sixty. Yet, all his hair had turned white. His blue eyes regarded Nevada.

"My boss took out a loan on the ranch a few months back and now the time is up. I was wondering since you have worked with the bank before if you could enlighten me on what to do."

"How long do you have?"

"A month."

"How about you come around on Sunday, so we can discuss it in detail? We could ask the Farm Debt Mediation board to review your stay, which could hold off proceedings from 30-120 days. In the interim, I'll talk with the bank manager and see what we can do."

"That would be great, sir. I'll see you Sunday."

"Definitely."

Nevada turned toward his truck.

"I hear all you're doing on the ranch. Keep the fire burning, son."

"Thank you, sir."

Until he figured something out, he wasn't planning to mention the loan to Amy just yet.

He couldn't add to her burden.

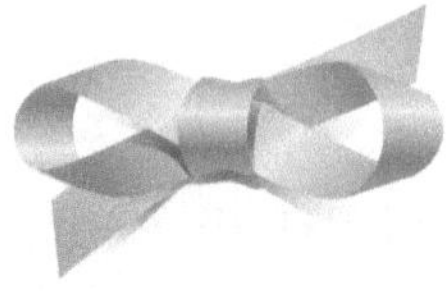

Chapter Twelve

Amy felt morose. Poor sleep was taking its toll, but the guilt wouldn't let up. She dreaded leaving. What if her dad woke up? A heavy sigh escaped.

She had just returned from the hospital but, instead of going off to sleep, restless energy looking for an outlet had her walking into the den.

Closing herself in, she sat down on the chair her father usually sat in. He'd take her on *Black Knight,* and when they returned, she'd ride home on his shoulders. How did those times change? She used to love running in the green grass and feeding the chickens.

It wouldn't do to dwell there.

As much as she wanted to turn back the hand of time, she couldn't change the past, and that's what it was, the past. *Easier said than done.*

She dug through the desk drawer, going over document after document. Like the ledger, most entries weren't in her father's writing. She assumed it was Nevada's. His beautiful cursive jumped out at her. Why wasn't she surprised that the writing would reflect the man?

Running down the records, she didn't know anything about the ranch, but she had enough knowledge to interpret a profit and loss record.

She gave a mental eye roll. As her father's only child, the ranch would invariably fall to her. In a matter of months, it would come crashing before her eyes like a castle in the empty air. Cliche, but true. She went through one drawer and started on another. Anything to keep her awake.

Nevada kept meticulous records. She'd give him that.

She flipped another page of a journal. An envelope lay nestled in its pages. Curious, she took out the note and perused it. Amy frowned. A demand letter requiring loan payment? She did a quick count down on the date.

Why did Dad need a loan? The new buildings? What a harebrained idea!

A guest ranch in a laid-back small town.

How viable was that?

Whatever. She wasn't going to have to deal with— Her cell phone rang. She checked the ID, Mel. "Hey."

"Hey to you. You didn't bother to call. Is that fair?"

Amy laughed. "I should've. I'm sorry."

"Yeah, I know." Mel's voice sounded subdued. "How's your dad?"

Amy swept a hand back to hold her hair out of her face. She didn't have energy to do anything to it, but Sam had insisted on helping her comb it out, so she just left it down. "He's still in a coma. It's not good. Feels like he's shrinking before my eyes." Amy's voice cracked on the last words and tears choked her.

"I'll come out on Friday and see you. We could return together on Sunday."

"You don't have to."

"I insist, unless you have reasons for me not to." Mel laughed. "Like the gorgeous foreman you told me about."

She was trying to make Amy feel better. She couldn't help laughing. "I never said anything about being gorgeous. I told you we don't get along. Come on!"

"If that's the case, I'll come see for myself." Then Mel's voice got serious again. "You can't change what has happened over the years. I can imagine how you feel but I'm sure your father won't hold anything against you."

"I keep telling myself that. My head knows it, but my heart can't seem to think it possible."

Amy got up and walked to the window. Young calves jumped about in the distance. A number of ranch hands cleaned out stalls. She turned and leaned against the wall.

"How's Eric?"

"He's counting the days until he sees you," she said, giggling. "The guy's got it bad."

Amy snorted, eased from the wall, settled in a seat, and propped her boots up. "He thinks he does. I don't see myself as a settling-down kind of girl." Really? Her heart mocked her. How about all the flips her heart did when Nevada was near. Indulging her pastime of eye rolling, she told herself not to go there.

"That may not be your statement in the next couple of weeks if your foreman is as gorgeous as my imagination tells me."

"Your imagination is sure running wild, my dear."

"Tell me he's not good looking."

"He is, but I'd be the last person on his mind. Not that I'm interested either. "

"That bad? Look, I got to go. Your boss is coming. See you in two days."

"He's yours, too. See you." She clicked off and took her seat.

Her phone went off again. *Lorraine.* Amy's heart stopped then beat at a painful staccato.

"Lorraine?" Her voice sounded breathless and she took a deep breath.

"Okay, don't panic. Can you get to the hospital? Your father suffered a cardiac arrest. I mean he had a heart attack. He's stable now, but we'd like to run some tests."

"I'll be there right away." Her legs hit the ground, and she made a short run to the back of the house where Sam was preparing the flower bed. "I need to get to the hospital." Amy's words came in short gasps.

Sam straightened, concern in her eyes.

"Call Nevada. He's around somewhere."

"I can drive myself." Amy turned to go, but a gentle hand stopped her.

"Not in this state. Reach him on his cell phone. It would be quicker that way."

"I don't have his..." Sweat dripped down her back. Her belly churned. *God, please.*

"Come with me." They ran around the house to the kitchen. Sam removed her gloves, picked up her cell phone, dialed Nevada's number, and passed the phone to Amy.

Her gaze flew to Sam's. Sam gave a quick nod.

With trembling hands, Amy put the phone to her ear.

. . ⚜ . .

THE ANNOYING VIBRATION started again. Nevada removed his gloves and fished the phone from his pocket. Sam's name came on the screen.

He frowned, accepting the call. "Sam?"

"It's not Sam." There was fear in her voice.

"Amy?"

"Yes, it's dad. He's..." she sniffled.

He turned in the direction of the ranch house.

"Calm down and talk to me." Covering the mouthpiece, he hollered to Dial. "I need to get to the hospital."

Then back on the phone. "I'm on my way. Is Sam there with you?" His legs ate the distance in large chunks.

"Yes, she is."

"Great. I'll be there in a few minutes." When the call ended, he ran the rest of the way.

Amy's eyes were red.

He felt pity for her. "Let me get out of these work clothes. You can tell me what they said on our way."

She nodded. He ran up the stairs, his brain working overtime. Was Anthony okay? What had happened? He prayed this wasn't the end for his dear friend.

• • ❧ • •

AMY WAS GRATEFUL THAT he'd come quickly and was even more touched by the fact that he cared that someone was with her. She sat wringing her hands, willing him to drive faster. He seemed to be lost in thought after she gave him Lorraine's information. Even Sam was quiet, but her comforting arm around Amy's shoulders eased her fright a bit.

She wished she could pray.

The fifteen-minute drive was the longest she'd ever had. A sigh of relief whooshed from her when he finally turned into the parking lot.

"Go on up, let me see if the doctor is around," Nevada said.

Amy nodded, grateful for Sam's support. Amy hugged herself as they walked up to the nurse's station. Sam told the nurses why they had come and led Amy on feet she didn't feel like were her own.

Amy would've rushed in there if fear of what she would see didn't hold her captive. Sam's gentle push urged her beyond the door into the hospital room. Amy gasped. Her father looked gray, like death was just waiting to take him.

"I'm sorry. I had to call you." Lorraine was documenting on Dad's chart.

"It's okay," Amy said absently, her gaze fleeing from her dad to Sam and back. Amy knelt beside him and took his hand, her heart thudding heavily like it bore a heavy weight.

"He's on a respirator." Lorraine's voice pierced the dense fog that surrounded her brain.

"His hands are cold," she said, looking at Lorraine.

"The room is warm enough now, and he's well covered. He should warm up soon. I'll leave you for now. When you're ready, I'll be at the nurses' station. I'll explain the tests to you."

Amy nodded and turned back to her father. She let her tears flow freely. The soft click of the door a second time told her someone else had entered, but she didn't look up.

"Please forgive me and don't die."

• • ❧ • •

HER WORDS CUT THROUGH Nevada like a knife. Sam stood close to the wall weeping quietly. He held her briefly, then squeezed her shoulders and walked to Amy. He knelt down beside her, silent.

He could see changes in the man, changes that told him it was only a matter of days. Nevada leaned his elbows on his thighs and fought his own tears.

He'd thought several times that maybe if he'd gone searching earlier, things would've been different.

Would he ever get to thank this man who had treated him like a son?

He started when Amy turned into him. Recovering from his shock, he put his arm around her and held her, stroking her hair as she cried, every wracking sob twisting the knife in his heart.

What did you say when you knew the end had come? The doctor was dealing with another emergency, but with what Nevada was seeing before him now... He didn't see the need if the tests wouldn't bring Anthony back.

Life was full of its own ups and downs, he thought as Amy cried into his shirt.

He feared the next few days would tilt her life off balance.

God, help us here.

Chapter Thirteen

Amy plunked onto the bed, giggling as her friend turned in a slow circle. The laughter sounded nice. Her father had been stable for two days. Even though she wanted to stay at the hospital, she had to come home because of Mel.

"You don't say. I'm actually on a ranch."

"Mmm-hmm." Amy set Mel's bag down and pulled off her boots. Mel finally dropped onto the bed.

"How come you get to enjoy all this by yourself?"

Amy snorted. "Tell me you're jealous and I'll tell you everything that will chase you away before you can blink." She counted off on her fingers. "No manicures and pedicures, no movies and parties..."

Mel smacked Amy and they landed on their backs, giggling.

"How about your sizzling cowboy? He's a man of few words but he has this...." Mel gave a dramatic sigh.

Amy felt a stirring in her heart. Nevada had breached her defenses, and she wasn't sure what to do about it. Despite his busy schedule, he dropped her off at the hospital, and still went to pick up Mel, only because Amy asked.

"Looks like I lost you there."

"He's not my cowboy. He's just my father's employee." She raised herself on one elbow. She wanted to say that everything was duty for him. But was it?

Why did she feel unhappy that he did everything for her only because he thought that a ranch hand had to? She applied mental brakes.

What did she expect? That he would say he did all of that out of love? Maybe for her father but for her? It was next to no chance at all. Shaking the disappointment, she laughed. "Let me show you around."

"Okay then," Mel said.

They walked hand in hand out of the ranch house into the midday sunshine. "There's something I want to check out. I haven't had time to do so and this time is about as good as any."

"What are the buildings for?" Mel asked as they got closer.

"Guest houses." They were cabin style and only one out of the four was incomplete. Amy led her friend into the larger of the buildings. If the plan worked it may not have been a bad idea, Amy thought as they went from one building to another.

"Your father wants to start something like a dude ranch?" There was awe in Mel's voice.

"I doubt it was my father's idea. Maybe Nevada's. All the documents I saw on the project were written by him. At least, I know they're not in Dad's writing."

Next, Amy took Mel to the new bunkhouse. It was mostly complete, but no fittings yet. Fifteen minutes later, they stepped back out.

"What's over there?"

"The maternity barn. Want to see it?"

"You bet."

Mel's enthusiasm didn't rub off on Amy, because at the back of her mind, this was the place she lost everything that mattered—Mom, her father's love.

Anyway, there was always novelty for the one who had never been to a place like this. Unlike her, who spent twenty-one years here and with all the memories involved. The rest of the tour passed in silence, Mel enjoying the scenery and Amy's thoughts not straying too far from her father. "Can we head to the house? I think I'm getting tired."

Mel draped a hand over Amy's and she struggled not to give in to the tears that hung constantly just beneath the surface. Thinking about her father had spoiled her day. She sighed deeply. Amy gave her friend a wan smile when Mel squeezed her shoulder.

Why did she sense that her world was about to be tilted from its balance?

• • ❧ • •

AMY AND HER FRIEND walked towards the house. Nevada had seen them at the new buildings earlier. What did she think? He wished he was there to know her thoughts about the project. Talks about the things he was doing on the ranch were far between. Their times together consisted of going to the hospital.

He was surprised to know he wanted her opinion. He continued rubbing his horse down. He'd gone to pick up her friend because Amy asked him.

A realization hit him. He'd do anything for her.

Was he setting himself up for another heartbreak?

I'm only doing my job.

Who was he kidding? Maybe the first few days, yes, and he'd told her so in no uncertain terms. Now he wasn't so sure. They both knew he wasn't under any obligation to do things for her, yet he did.

What about the day he took her shopping for clothes and Sam's groceries? Even that time he didn't have to. Angel could drive, so could Dial. The second ranch truck had been fixed.

"Hey, boss," Dial called in greeting, as he led his horse into the stall.

Nevada snapped out of his musing. "Dial, how is the work coming?"

"I feel every one of my muscles." He chuckled, a twinkle in his eyes.

At this time, everyone felt the effect of the trips around the maternity barn and cleaning up the place. Even the horses were easier to catch for work. "That's how you know you're alive."

They all enjoyed the work. That was the only way anyone would last on the ranch. Dial was no exception. He loved the job, especially the horses. He was good with them. The young guy was a born rancher.

"True, boss. I'll miss it here when I go back to school."

"And we'll miss you too. It's a good thing you'll be here till this calving is over. I can't afford to have one less hand at this time."

"How's the big boss?"

"Not ..." Nevada's cell phone rang and he unclipped it from his belt. The ID showed the hospital.

His heart beat double time. Why were they calling him? Where was Amy? He accepted the call and placed it to his ear. "Hello?"

"This is Daisy from Blue Song General. Can you get to the hospital right away? We're not able to get Amy on her phone."

"How is Anthony?"

"Not good." He didn't miss the sadness in the nurse's voice. Nevada turned on his heels. "I'm heading out to the hospital, Dial," he said over his shoulder.

Without waiting for a response, he ran across the field towards the ranch house to find Amy. "Where is your phone?" he asked as he bounded into the kitchen breathless.

"Oh, in my room." Her wide-eyed gaze searched his. "What's the matter?" she asked, coming to her feet. Mel rose, too.

"It's your father. We need to get to the hospital now." He turned to her friend. "Mel, can you find Sam? Tell her to get Angel handy, in case they need to meet us at the hospital."

Mel gave her friend a quick hug and a pat on her back. "Go on, Amy."

Once in the truck, Nevada threw it into reverse and stepped on the gas. As he turned onto the hospital road minutes later, he prayed. That was all he'd done for the last couple of days. That Anthony would have a miracle. But Daisy's voice told him this wasn't it. "What happened to your phone?"

"I left it in my room."

Nevada remembered she had said that. He kept his eyes on the road.

Fear clawed up his belly, squeezing his heart till he was sure it would stop beating. Along with it was anger at her for not thinking she should keep her phone close by at all times. But getting upset wouldn't change anything.

Maneuvering into the parking lot sooner than he normally would have, he pushed the gear to park and climbed down. He marched across the parking area into the hospital.

Nevada held the elevator door for Amy. Seeing her wide-eyed stare, his anger deflated. He reached out and squeezed her hand.

When the elevator dinged to a stop, Nevada was out in a flash and made a short walk to the room Anthony occupied.

• • ❧ • •

AMY RAN AFTER HIM, feeling numbed by fear. She wasn't sure about the frequency of irregularity her heart was beating with. She tried to pray but the words stuck in her throat.

She stumbled in just as the doctor covered her father's face. The doctor swung his stethoscope over his neck. "I'm sorry, Miss Jayden. We did all we could."

Amy ran to the bed and yanked off the cloth. "No, you can't die, Dad. Please wake up. Wake up." She pleaded, shaking him.

His face was peaceful. Was this the end? Her heart pounded, her pulse roaring in her ears. Why would he not wake up even once? Why did she not have the chance to ask for forgiveness? Why had she let the past fester until it was too late?

She screamed and crumpled to the floor, sobs wracking her body. Amy held a hand to her chest to keep her heart from splitting into bits like it was bent on doing.

Nevada squatted beside her, his hand on her shoulder. "Amy, I'll be back." He hesitated a little and then rose and left with the doctor.

Daisy tried to talk to Amy but not one word penetrated her ears. She stared at her Dad. *Was this truly the end?* She thought again. She wouldn't see or talk to her dad. If only she could undo the years...

Amy burst into tears afresh.

After what felt like forever, Nevada walked in with two men in tow. He squatted beside her like he'd done earlier. "Amy, these men are taking your dad's body to the morgue until we make plans."

"Don't let them take him away," she cried, grabbing his shirt.

"You know the hospital can't leave him here indefinitely and keeping him won't bring him back."

She looked from him to the men who were there to take her father away, torn between letting them go or not.

Amy pressed shaky hands to her face and cried like she hadn't done in years.

Chapter Fourteen

Nevada's heart melted at the anguish in Amy's eyes and he gathered her into his arms. Once he entered and saw all the gadgets disconnected, he'd realized that moment, Anthony was gone from them forever. The doctor said he was sorry. Everyone was always sorry when someone died.

His anger stirred again and he pushed it away. It was no one's fault what happened to Anthony.

Lord help us. He prayed. *The next couple of days will be rough on everyone. Lord, please grant Amy strength. Set her free from the guilt that has held her bound.*

When the gurney was wheeled out, she started crying afresh. Nevada, helpless and filled with his own grief, let her cry as silent tears coursed down his own cheeks.

The man he had come to see as his own father was gone forever.

Later that night, Nevada sat in the den trying to update the ledger, but his concentration kept slipping to the events of the day. He glanced up to see Amy resting against the door jamb. He hadn't heard her.

He rose. "Amy? Were you able to rest?"

"No," she said shortly.

She pushed past him and went to the table, leaning against it.

He assessed her disheveled hair and puffy face and he ached for her. She was a far cry from the young woman who'd come to the ranch a mere two weeks ago. "We could ask the doctor to give you something to help you sleep."

"I don't need sleep."

"Amy, you can't go on like this."

"When were you planning to tell me about the loan?"

"What?" He frowned. How did she know?

"I told you I wanted to know what's going on here."

Nevada knew grief when he saw it. Amy was spoiling for a fight and he wasn't going to grant her that. "We can talk about this when you're in a better—"

"Don't patronize me, Nevada. Were you planning to tell me?"

He dropped into the chair he'd just vacated and rubbed his stubble. *Give me wisdom, Lord.*

"I'm talking to you, Nevada."

She was still talking quietly but he could feel the heat of her emotion bubbling beneath. "Amy, I heard you the first time. I didn't know about the loan until the bank manager sent the notification demanding payment."

"And what's the plan?"

"I talked with Angel's dad and we went to see the manager. He said if I could come up with fifty percent, he'd give us a few weeks extension considering the issues on the ground."

"And how much are we looking at?"

She was quizzing him like he had something to hide. "I talked to your dad's accountant and we were able to arrange some payment for—"

"And all that behind my back."

"Amy, can you drop this? You're grieving and you don't need the extra stress."

"I'm not dropping it."

He rose. "Your choice. I'm not going to sit down here and argue over things we could talk over nicely."

Her face crumpled but she regained herself. She turned and walked away. "Amy?" She stopped but didn't turn.

Nevada walked up to her. He tilted up her chin. "I'm not trying to keep anything from you. You had too much to deal with and I didn't want to bother you."

"I'm sorry." She sniffed. "I want to do something."

"Don't be sorry, Amy. And you will have plenty of time to do things. Let's get you to Sam. The interment is tomorrow. You need all your strength."

He could sense her shaking. She needed rest. He didn't like this dry-eyed grief, wasn't sure which was better. But he knew girls cried when they were unhappy. He wished she would, instead of keeping the hurt in.

• • ❧ • •

THE NEXT MORNING, NEVADA took in the solemn faces of those who stood in front of the barn that served as the meeting area. Angel's father stood beside his wife who was seated under the shade of the big oak.

The Doyles' were there too and all the ranch hands, fifteen of them. Amy sat crying silently, flanked by Mel and Sam. Despite her blotchy red face, she looked stunning in the black dress she wore, her hair flowing down her back.

The reverend droned on about the good life Anthony had lived. At funerals, eulogies were said which sometimes were not the truth, maybe because no one wanted to speak ill of the dead, but everything the good reverend said about Anthony was true. None of them would say the man had treated them badly.

"No matter what we do on earth, only that which we do for the Lord shall stand. Jesus said, 'Inasmuch as you did it to the least of these ones you did it for me.'"

Nevada examined his heart and his motives for everything he did. As he stood in that cool morning breeze—even nature seemed to know that there was mourning in the air—he surrendered his heart to the Lord again asking God to help him.

The casket laid open. Everyone passed and laid flowers as a mark of their deep respect. The last part of the interment was done in silence and then everyone converged to the barn for light refreshments.

"How are you feeling?" he asked Angel's mom.

"Mostly fine, just a little tired."

Nevada hugged her. "I'm glad you're doing okay. The color is back in your face."

"Thanks, son. We need to pay our respect to Amy before we head out."

Pastor Rodriguez engulfed Nevada in a hug. "Keep your eyes on the Lord, son. You'll need that in the next few days because everyone will be relying on you," he said and they were gone.

Angel must have told his dad all that'd been going on.

Feeling sullen, Nevada walked towards the calving lot.

· · ⚬⚬ · ·

AMY'S HEAD POUNDED from so much crying. Her cheek muscles ached from trying to keep up the smile she didn't feel like, yet gave everyone.

Mel had left for the airport immediately after Amy's dad had been buried. She needed to catch her flight back to LA. Her departure further plunged Amy into whatever it was she seemed to be falling into. She also needed to call her boss, but couldn't summon the strength just yet. Feeling bereft, she sat on the sofa and accepted the condolences from people who didn't make the funeral.

Sam was overseeing refreshments for their friends. Though she should be out helping, she couldn't will herself to do anything. The poor woman had baked for the better part of the night in preparation for today and all Amy did was mope.

Worse still, she seemed to have alienated Nevada with her display last night. She looked around wishing her father would walk in and say it was all a lie.

There was a slight knock and an elderly couple walked in. Angel's parents. Sam had introduced them when they came for one of the services. She got up and pasted a smile on her face.

"I'm sorry for your loss," Consuela said, coming to hug Amy.

The tears that clogged the back of her throat threatened to break through. Would she ever be able to stop crying?

The woman looked frail, not like the first time Amy met her. Had Consuela been sick? "Thank you," Amy said trying to keep her voice steady.

The tall man so much like Angel gave his own condolences. Obviously, a man of few words. They left shortly afterwards.

After about half an hour, when nobody else came, she assumed everyone had left. She came into the kitchen and met Sam washing the dishes and cups that'd been used. "I know I should be helping you out, except that I just can't get..." She choked on the words.

Sam's eyes filled with compassion. "Don't worry, Amy dear. No one is expecting anything from you."

She nodded swallowing past the lump in her throat. "I'll be out back then."

"Okay. I'll get into town briefly to pick up a few things. I've used up everything in the house. If you need anyone, Nevada will be out somewhere. You can reach him on the phone."

Amy nodded again and stepped out.

She wasn't his responsibility. He had things to do.

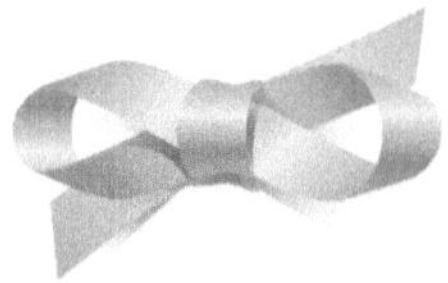

Chapter Fifteen

"Where's Amy?" Nevada asked as he came in behind Sam. "Maybe in her room. I haven't checked."

He nodded and sat on the stool beside the worktable. He dragged one of the grocery bags in and pulled out a cold pop. "Can I have one of these?

"Sure. Pass one to me."

Shaking some of the condensation from the can, he opened it and took a swig. He sighed as bubbly coldness trickled down his throat. Nevada closed his eyes and ran a hand back through his hair.

"I need to check on Amy."

"Go ahead," he said, getting up. He took another pull of his drink and started to unpack the groceries. Sam came back almost immediately.

"She's not in her room."

His hand stilled and he turned slowly to face Sam, his head inclined. Concern marred the woman's features. "She isn't in her room?"

"No." Nevada took a look at his watch. Four p.m. Where could she be? Another day just two weeks prior flashed in his mind. What if she wandered off the ranch? "Where do you think she'd be headed?"

"She went towards the back of the house earlier. I thought she would've returned in my absence. You could check the new barn first."

"All right. Please keep your phone handy. If she's not there, I won't come back here. I'll alert you. You can reach Angel and Dial at the maternity barn." He didn't wait for a response as he turned on his heels in the direction of the barn. If she wasn't there, he'd check the grave site. *God please keep her safe.*

He rounded the bend, walked into the barn, and almost tripped over her legs.

He breathed a sigh of relief. She was fast asleep, her neck in an awkward position. Had she been here since the funeral? He had not seen much of her after her father had been laid to rest. He thought she'd probably gone to her room. Had she even eaten anything? He hunched down and pushed her hair from her face. Damp tendrils were stuck to her cheeks.

Away from the sun, her skin felt cold to touch. Nevada sighed. Lifting her gently, he was careful not to jar her even though he doubted she would wake up to anything. She snuggled close and sighed. Nevada's breath whooshed from him in response to the innocent act and fast on its heels was pity for the woman in his arms.

He strode in the direction of the house, marveling at how light she felt in his arms.

Sam must've seen them through the kitchen window because she came to the door and let him in.

"She hasn't eaten all day."

Nevada nodded. He thought as much. Maneuvering up the steps was no easy feat. He pushed open her door and getting to the bed, he knelt with one knee and laid her gently on it. She turned to her side and continued sleeping. Days of sitting with her father through the night had taken their toll.

Nevada removed her boots half expecting her to wake, but she didn't. What woman did this to herself? No food or rest all day, she must be bone weary. He took the stool beside her bed and sat down. Before he could analyze what he was doing, he reached out, flicked the hair from her face and rubbed a few strands between his fingers. Soft. He took his hand away and let his gaze roam the room.

He'd never entered here, only the master bedroom on occasions when Anthony asked to see him there.

Grief took Nevada by surprise. He missed the man. Pushing the feeling away, he took in the whole room. There was nothing frilly-girly about her room. A table and chair sat under the window overlooking the artificial lake.

Except for the rose water perfume that hung over the room like a curtain, you'd doubt it was a girl's room. His brows met northward. What did it say of the woman? Sophisticated, yet practical. On the other hand, if one considered the near masculinity in the room, it showed something else. Did she love being in control?

"Is she still sleeping?" Sam's voice came quietly at the door and Nevada started like someone caught red-handed with meat from the soup pot.

Nodding, he stood and rubbed his hands on his jeans. He slipped past Sam and went out. The girl was stirring a myriad of emotions in him, emotions he'd refused to analyze. Was he ready to let himself be vulnerable or feel that kind of pain again?

$$\cdot \ \cdot \ \infty \ \cdot \ \cdot$$

THE NEXT DAY, AMY STAYED cooped up in her room. It was easier that way because everything on the ranch was a reminder of her dad. She wondered how she got to her room last night and came up with only one logical explanation. Nevada.

Her phone rang. Eric.

She accepted the call.

"Mel told me. I'm sorry for your loss."

"Thanks." Her throat tickled again. "I'll need some more time to tie up loose ends."

He was silent for a moment. "Sure."

When the call ended, she switched off the phone.

A knock sounded on her door. Amy frowned. Who would that be? Sam? "Come in."

The door opened and Nevada stuck his head around it. "Can I talk with you for a sec?"

Amy nodded.

When she reached the door, she leaned against the jamb, holding the knob in her right hand.

His hazel eyes regarded her. Amy fought the flush that made its way up her neck. She was sure she looked a sight—her hair not having seen a comb in two days. All she had the strength to do was bathe and throw on some clothes.

"I was thinking of something."

"What's that?"

"Are you up for a little ride? I want to take you somewhere."

Amy closed her eyes.

"It won't be long. Promise."

"All right."

He smiled. "Grab a jacket and meet me in the kitchen."

Ten minutes later, they had their horses saddled and rode into the evening. Nevada carried a basket in front of him, but she didn't ask what was in it. The sight of food nauseated her. Even hunger pangs couldn't lure her to eat.

Amy wrapped her jacket tighter. The frigid air mimicked the chill in her heart and reminded her that her father was gone forever. The best thing was just to sell off the place, make sure Sam and everyone was well settled and get back to her life.

When they reached the edge of the ranch, Nevada dismounted, setting the basket down. Amy climbed down too.

He offered his hand. Amy slipped hers in it and loved the way her small hand fit into his.

Nevada led her to the small creek. It had thawed. This was one place she had loved to come with Dad. And Mom too, when she was alive. They'd had several picnics here with friends.

"This is my favorite place. I love to come here when I need to think and pray." He chuckled. "Not often, with the work that needs to be done."

"My parents and I used to come here—" Amy's throat closed.

Nevada turned her around and held her. "God didn't create us in isolation for a purpose, so we can offer each other strength, support."

"I don't deserve anybody's help." She tasted the salt of tears.

"Don't say that, Amy." He cupped her face and stared into her eyes. "None of us deserves anything God ever gives us. But He gives it anyway."

He thumbed away her tears then held her again.

The thumping of his heart soothed her, his arms feeling like a shield against the onslaught of the emotion she struggled with.

Amy wrapped her arms around him and held while she cried. "I'm supposed to be strong."

"You are. You lost your dad, so we understand that you don't feel like having company, don't feel like eating. But you're strong and will be fine."

After what felt like forever, he set her away. "I need you to eat a little food. And don't say no." His voice was firm even though his eyes were gentle. He smiled and chucked her on the chin.

Amy gave him a wobbly smile.

Nevada grabbed the blanket from the basket and laid it on the bare ground. He handed her a shawl to keep her warm then set the plate of enchiladas in front of her. Pouring some orange juice in a glass cup, he set it beside the food.

Her stomach rumbled and Nevada smiled. "Sam said it's your favorite, so let's see you do justice to it."

"You're not eating?"

"No. Eat as much as you can."

Amy dug into the food. She sensed Nevada's gaze on her and looked up. Their gaze held and everything seemed to come to a standstill.

He reached out and tucked her hair behind her ear. "You're beautiful, Amy."

Her face flamed. Was he flattering her? When she looked in the mirror, all she saw was a stranger. "Thanks," she choked out. "And for yesterday."

"Don't give it any thought." His knuckles brushed her cheek, lingered a few seconds then dropped away. "Eat up, so we can head back."

Swallowing, she nodded. Was she falling for Nevada?

Chapter Sixteen

Life on the ranch had lulled into routine during the days following Anthony's funeral. Nevada went to the construction site to talk to the workers. He had less than three weeks to come up with money to repay the loan to keep the bank from taking over the ranch.

How did it come to this? Anthony must've had plans, but Nevada didn't have a way of knowing now.

He talked with the lead guy and then walked into the completed cabins, moving through the rooms. *Lord, my heart trusts in You and I am helped. I won't give up, help me trust You as You show us the way through this.*

They'd stop work until the loan was settled. While they were at it, he needed to come up with a plan fast so that everything wouldn't fall through.

He stepped out into the sunshine and went through the other cabins. When all this was over, he'd have not a single doubt as to how God brought them through.

He turned toward the ranch and glimpsed a red sports car in front of the ranch house.

Did Amy have a visitor?

As he came closer, he noted that whoever owned the car was nowhere in sight. Discarding his boots at the door, he went into the house. Voices came from the den. He felt propelled towards them. Whatever this was about, it wasn't a social meeting. After a quick rap, he poked his head through the door.

Nevada took in everything in a quick snap. The ranch ledgers lay open between Amy and an older man.

Nevada frowned.

So soon? Her father had only been gone one week and now this? "What's going on here?" he asked, walking fully into the room.

"Nevada, meet Mr. Dylan. He's a property agent. Mr. Dylan, this is the ranch's foreman."

She said 'the ranch' like it was nothing. Nevada took the proffered hand and then turned to her. "Amy, can I talk with you for a second?"

"After I'm done here. It won't take long."

"Amy, it's just a week—"

She closed her eyes. "Please, don't say it."

"Anthony wouldn't want you to do this," he tried again.

"So, you think you know my father so well?" she asked.

Did she think this was about him? What memory would be left of the man who had built his life on this? Nevada knew she'd sell eventually, but just not this soon. "Can we talk about this?"

"Nevada, I'm glad you like this place and want to keep it going. But once I get a buyer, I'm selling. If the new owner wants you to stay on, that's fine."

"Amy, you think this is about me?" He kept his tone even.

She came to stand in front of him, arms folded across her chest. "You tell me. It's really frustrating talking to you when you won't put your thoughts into words."

"I think you should talk about this," Mr. Dylan said from where he stood, a few steps away from them.

"Mr. Dylan," Nevada gave him a small smile. "The ranch is not for sale. At least, not yet. I think there's been some misunderstanding."

"That's not the impression Ms. Jayden gave me."

"How about we get back to you?" Nevada asked, his gaze on Amy. Her nostrils flared. He expected her to contradict him.

Papers rustled behind them.

"Just go ahead with what you have and give me a call," Amy said.

"You two should talk it over and, Ms. Jayden, give me a call."

"What's this about, Nevada Logan?" She asked the moment the older man left. Her eyes stared daggers at him.

"Amy, what do you know about labor? Nothing. If you're selling a year, maybe six months from now, I'd have held my peace. Do you have no respect for your father's memory?"

She flinched and Nevada gentled his tone. "Talk to your dad's lawyer. I don't have any right to stop you, but I'd think you would want to wait a little longer."

"Why would I? Tell me."

Counting to ten, he spoke quietly. "You say I don't speak my mind. But does anything I have said make sense to you?"

She stood there looking at him for a moment and he wondered what was going on in her mind.

"It does. But you know you won't change my mind."

"I know."

After a moment, she walked back to the seat she'd just vacated and sat down. Nevada pushed the door closed and came to sit opposite her. A few minutes of tense silence passed. He had to say something. "Amy, I know how you feel about this place," he said, jerking his thumb behind him. "With good reasons, I grant you that. But can you just hold on for a few more months? Let these buildings be completed, let's wean these new calves. Even if you decide to go ahead and sell, it will be worth more. Let me show you the land is worth keeping, but if in another four to six months you think otherwise, then sell."

Amy chewed her cheek in contemplation. Logically, she couldn't argue with that, could she?

"What's in it for you?" she asked.

"If I can keep your dad's legacy like I think he would want, I'd have succeeded at something."

As for his feelings for her, it was a pipe dream. Amy couldn't wait to get out of there.

. . ⤫ . .

SOMETHING FLASHED IN his eyes. Maybe pain, and then it was gone. Was that all?

If she put her sentiments aside, he did well with the ranch. Why did he think he had to do this, to show he could? What happened to make him unsure of himself? Who did he want to prove something to, himself or someone else?

She looked at him and he stared right back. Her heart stirred. She'd give him the chance and hope things worked out. "How do you hope to clear the loan?" she asked, her hand waving over the letter on the ledger still sitting open in front of her.

"I have another meeting with the accountant at the end of the week. We'll come up with something."

"Three weeks." She stood up and walked to the door. Easing it open, she looked out. She was having problems thinking straight when he looked at her with those eyes.

What happened to her resolve to sell? She had no reason to refuse, did she? Coming back, she stood beside him. Gentleman that he was, he stood up, too. "I'm leaving for LA the day after tomorrow. I don't know how soon I'll be back. You have from now until next week to come up with a solid plan. If you can do that, then I'll hold off selling for now. Is that fair enough?"

His lopsided smile lightened his eyes. He was like a child who had seen Santa Claus for the first time. Her heart melted and she found she was almost crying. She was glad she'd agreed. Whatever it meant to him, she'd let him discover.

His hands came together as though in prayer. "Thank you, Amy." He was still smiling.

Her phone rang and he signaled to her and walked away.

Chapter Seventeen

Nevada returned to the ranch house to grab his dinner before heading to the new bunkhouse. Deciding there was no need to continue to stay at the ranch house, he'd packed his things.

Amy sat on the glider in her favorite spot.

He made a detour and came to her. Looked like they'd made good progress since their talk last night. "You're not sleeping?"

"Not yet."

He sat with her and set the glider in motion.

"This place feels quiet in a strange way. I don't think I'll ever get used to it again."

Nevada took her hand and threaded his fingers through hers. "Give yourself time. It heals wounds."

"Did yours heal? Have you ever wondered who your parents are?" She glanced at him. "Uh, I'm sorry. You don't have to answer that."

"I'll always wonder about that all my life. But if they didn't think I was worth it, then, I don't pine away for them. Life on the street, sleeping in the subway made me strong."

"I always loved this place, until mom died. I never saw my parents argue and may never understand what happened that day." She sighed. "Mom always had a temper. But she was an amazing person. Dad understood her. I always told myself I would have their kind of love someday."

"And now?"

"I don't know. I guess I still want that. What about you?"

He chuckled. "I met this girl last year and we hung out when we could. I thought we had started to build a relationship. Long story short, I was sadly mistaken."

He didn't want to repeat Brooke's words. She'd called him a failure. Words he tried not to take to heart, but it wasn't easy.

Amy let the matter drop. Which was good. She stirred things in his heart and he had it bad for her. But that was his secret for now.

Staying at the bunkhouse would help his resolve. As long as she intended to sell, she wasn't planning to stick around. What skills did he have to live in her world? Next to none.

She leaned against him. "How's your place? Isn't it cold, still?"

"I use the mobile heater." Nevada draped his arm around her and she snuggled closer.

"Why did you decide to move?"

He shrugged. "No reason."

She sighed. "Here we go again. There's a reason for everything we do. You probably don't want to tell me. Is it so hard—"

Nevada turned and cupped her cheek. He leaned down and pressed his lips against hers and then withdrew. "Is that reason enough?"

She stared at him, her eyes wide.

Nevada held her gaze, giving her time to move away.

He kissed her again. Briefly. He breathed. "Amy, I can't be in the same house with you and not act on my feelings. Does that satisfy your curiosity now?"

She nodded.

Nevada dropped his hand.

"I think you should go home," she said smiling.

I'm home. Amy, I'm home. "Good advice. See you in the morning."

If he didn't leave, he would kiss her again against everything he'd told himself.

. . ✽ . .

THE AROMA OF CINNAMON filled the kitchen as Amy brought out the first batch of cookies Sam was baking. "I won't be leaving to-morrow," she said to Sam.

Nevada watched her when she wasn't looking. After her capitulation yesterday, he'd been ecstatic. Somehow, something had shifted in him. And the kiss last night... It was meant to shut her up, but then, what he said was true.

As he looked at her, he thought. Was he the only one affected by their kiss? "Why, that's good." Nevada heard himself say.

A pink hue crept into her cheeks. "I mean you get to stay around one more day," he said inanely and watched the color deepen. Nevada wanted to flog himself. Why did he have to embarrass her?

"Your boss is bound to flip this time," Sam said, coming to their rescue.

"I called him. He's upset and I understand. I'm not sure how soon I'll be back to tie up loose ends."

Like put the ranch up for sale. He sighed. Allowing his heart to get involved was just going to get it broken and trampled upon.

"The lawyer called to say he was coming tomorrow," Amy said.

"Oh, okay then." Nevada picked up his and Sam's plates and carried them to the sink.

"He requested that you be there, Nevada."

Frowning, he turned; the apples he'd removed from the fridge in hand. He wasn't family, why should he be there? "Did he say why?"

She gave him a careless shrug. "He didn't say."

She got up too and picked up her plate. Nevada caught Sam's look and shrugged, giving her an I-don't-know-why-I-should-be-there look.

"What time is the meeting?"

"Nine a.m. He also requests that you be there, Sam."

Nevada realized Amy was looking at him instead of Sam. Did she think he knew why the man wanted him to be present?

"Do you already know what's in the will?" she asked.

"Don't be ridiculous. Your father never discussed such a thing with me." He dropped the plate of apples on the table and folded his arms across his chest. Looked like for every step forward they made, they took two more backwards. "Why are you always suspicious of me?" The whole emotion was etched in her beautiful face. "So, you think I know something and that's why I was asking for you to hold off selling?"

Her raised brow said she didn't believe him. He reached past her, picked up the towel and wiped his hands. Dumping it on the table, he shook his head even though what he wanted to do was shake her. "Think what you want. I know I'm not family and don't have a part in this. Believe what you choose, I'll be at the meeting to hear what your father has to tell me, but be sure of one thing, I won't lay a finger on anything I haven't worked for."

With that he stepped past her and walked out.

• • ❧ • •

"I DON'T LIKE WHAT YOU are doing at all," Sam said.

Amy started to wash up the plates. What had she done?

"Why do you think your father trusted him? You haven't given him any chance at all. What exactly is your problem, young lady?"

Amy rinsed and dried the last plate. She'd hurt him. Shame washed over her. He'd been good to her every step of the way through her ordeal.

"I was just wondering why he needed to be at the reading of the will." Her voice sounded alien even to her.

"It's not sufficient reason to throw an accusation at him."

"Sam, come on. All I did was ask a simple question for goodness sake."

"Is that how you were taught to ask questions?" Sam asked, shaking her head as though disgusted. Amy's eyes smarted. Somehow, she thought he'd know something she didn't. If her dad kept things from her, whose fault was it?

"What happened to you, my dear child? Your father trusted this boy and loved him like a son." She came to Amy and placed a hand on her shoulder. "I'm sure he doesn't know anything. Besides, would it be so wrong if your father chose to reward him for all he's done since he came to work here? Even you wouldn't say no to that."

If Amy felt ashamed before, she felt it more now. Her face flamed. Now that she asked, she saw how stupid her question had been. Her throat tickled and her eyes felt gritty as though filled with sand.

"Give Nevada time to prove himself. But if you won't you'll have me to answer to."

Amy chanced a glance at Sam. She didn't look angry. Swallowing past the lump in her throat, she hugged Sam. "I'm sorry."

"It isn't me you should be telling. Tell Nevada."

Amy flushed. She couldn't face him just yet. "I will, but not now."

Sam patted her on her back. "I have some things to attend to. Don't forget to put the lights out when you turn in."

Amy cleaned up the kitchen and did her best to hang around and apologize. When the giant grandfather clock in the living room chimed eleven, she gave up. Maybe he was avoiding her, which was just as well.

She locked the back door and closed the one through the kitchen so that he could come in if he needed anything.

But she'd definitely find him in the morning.

Chapter Eighteen

Nevada walked toward the house on the dot of nine. His belly churned. He'd stayed away this long so that he wouldn't seem too eager. He prayed that whatever Anthony wrote in the will wouldn't be such that Nevada would look bad in Amy's eyes.

He shouldn't care, yet he couldn't help that he did. The lawyer hadn't come. At least, there was no car. Taking a few calming breaths, he entered the kitchen. The smell of cake wrapped around him and his stomach rumbled.

"Come help me with this," Sam said, gesturing to the flask of fresh fruit juice she'd prepared. He took it from her and put it in the fridge.

"You skipped breakfast." She thrusted a plate of fried potatoes in his hand. He looked at her and then turned away, reaching for the ketchup from the refrigerator. "I wasn't hungry."

"Really, or you didn't want to face Amy."

"Maybe that too, but really, I wasn't hungry."

A car pulled into the driveway. Nevada peered out the window. It was the lawyer. He got out of his BMW and walked toward the house. The oven timer went off and Sam turned to remove the cake she was baking.

"Go on, I'll meet you in the sitting room." As he turned to go, she put out a hand to stop him. "No matter what Amy says, promise me you won't be angry."

After a moment's hesitation he told her, "I won't."

She nodded and he left.

Nevada met the lawyer, greeted him, and showed him to the den.

Unease strapped like a band around his chest and stomach, and he wasn't sure why. He took a quick look in the direction of the wiry old man that sat to Nevada's right. He was the same lawyer Anthony had used in the five years Nevada had been at the ranch.

He thought of asking him why he had to be there but the move was squelched by Amy's appearance. Her flowery perfume filled the room, heightening Nevada's senses. She wore her hair—

Breaking his thought, which was determined to take inventory of how beautiful she looked in the tee-shirt that said *beauty plus brains,* and form fitting jeans, he leaned back on the chair, feigning an easiness he was far from feeling. Maybe if he wasn't under suspicion, he wouldn't be wound up tight like a malfunctioning clock.

"Good morning, Mr. Roberts," she said as she sashayed into the room. The older man stood and took her proffered hand. She then took her seat. She smiled at Nevada. He wasn't sure what to make of it.

He turned away. Sam wheeled in a tea trolley. Nevada stood up and went to help her. Giving him a wink and smile, she let him wheel it to the center of the den.

"A fine morning it is, Mr. Roberts, and thanks for coming."

"My pleasure ma'am," he took her hand and shook it firmly. "Anthony was more than a client to me. I'd do anything for him."

Amy rose from where she sat at the table and passed out the drinks and cookies. He looked at Sam and caught her expression. It was hard to interpret.

Amy handed him a glass and their fingers brushed. She colored immediately, a tad shade lighter than her hair.

"Thank you." He was glad his voice held strong.

"My pleasure," she stammered and went back to her seat. Nevada told himself not to look, but stare, he did.

"It's a pity I'm doing this so soon," the lawyer's clear voice brought Nevada back to the present.

He hoped no one noticed where his eyes had been. He'd almost forgotten he'd been on the hot seat, so to speak, because of her. He'd never seen her look so pretty with her long hair piled up on her head and a slender column of neck exposed. The redness of her face added a novelty to her look that made him long to kiss her. Again.

But, what did he have to offer? He tried to focus his scattered brain on the words of the man.

"A month ago, Anthony called me to this very room and told me he wanted to amend his will. At that time, I asked why he thought it was necessary. He laughed and said, "Death is the way of every soul that lived and no one knows his time." His words had caused a disquiet in me but I knew your father," Mr. Roberts said, his gaze directed to Amy. "As a man of great faith, if he wanted to amend his will then, he had good reason. Barely a few weeks later I heard he'd been in an accident."

Who told him? As though reading his thoughts he pointed to Sam. "This came as a surprise to me when Sam called. Anthony had lived here all his life, being the fourth generation to take over the ranch. My first reaction was, what in the world could've happened?"

The man seemed to struggle for a moment and then looked at each of them pointedly. "I'm glad he knew the Lord, because that is all that counts after all is said and done."

Nevada cast a glance at Amy. Her eyes swam and he noticed a mild trembling in the hands clasped in front of her. He itched to hold her in his arms and tell her all would be well.

Roberts cleared his throat as if remembering why he came. He picked up his portfolio and opened it.

Nevada's pulse skyrocketed. He passed the will to Amy. "Sealed and stamped," he said.

She looked at it and returned it to him. He then raised it for Nevada and Sam to see before he broke the seal.

He did it gently, as though out of reverence for his client and friend or the fact that this was going to change the lives of everyone involved.

He unfolded the paper and ran his eyes down the page. Nevada didn't think his heart could race any faster. He resisted the urge to rub clammy hands against his Wranglers. Was anyone else feeling that way?

"Sam." Roberts looked at her directly, and then read. "After my wife died, I thought everything would unravel with me feeling the impact of her death and the guilt I held onto. There was nothing I could do to erase the things we had said to each other. I couldn't see through the haze. Yet, you held everything together."

Roberts paused for a moment. "I don't know what we'd have done without you. You will be provided for, for the rest of your life. In the event that you choose to marry again I have worked it all out that you will continue to be supported. My lawyer will give you the details."

Nevada felt a huge weight on his chest as he watched the tears flow from her eyes. He didn't know will reading was an emotional thing—he'd never been to one. Roberts turned to Nevada and he sat up in the chair.

"Nevada, you have been more than a foreman to me. You have been the son I didn't have, single minded in your purpose and devotion to the land as you worked. It beat my imagination. I'm sure the guest ranch concept will work out fine. I'm hoping you'll agree to stay on in some capacity, even when I'm gone. I'm giving you a little piece of land north of the creek. My lawyer will provide you with the details."

Nevada felt his face drain of color. He couldn't look at Amy. Not what he planned. He was overwhelmed and humbled at the same time. He hadn't done anything to deserve this. He loved what he did and that was it.

Seest thou a man diligent in his works, he shall stand before kings and not mere men. The scripture breathed across his spirit. Was God rewarding him? For what? His struggle at trusting Him?

"Amy, I don't know what to say to you. I longed all my days to see you return home even if not to stay but to see me as a father who loves you and for you to see this place as home. I regret all the years we lost but I only hope you'll find it in your heart to forgive me. No one regretted your mother's death more than I. As much as I wished, I couldn't change all that has happened. I give you this whole ranch to do with as you wish."

Nevada looked at her and his heart fell to his toes. To do as she wished?

She was crying. Maybe guilt, maybe remorse over all her father had to say.

"On one condition," the man said, and Nevada's head snapped back to the lawyer. "I know you wouldn't hesitate to sell off the ranch, so I'm attaching a condition to your inheritance."

Even the man didn't seem in a hurry to impart the condition. Amy came out of her seat as though it had burned her.

"You can only inherit the land if you live here for at least three months. Nevada will manage the ranch in the interim. If in that course of time, you choose not to stay, then the ranch can be auctioned and the money given to charity."

His gaze darted between the two other people and then to Amy. Her eyes were closed, but tears slipped out.

Mr. Roberts went through the rest of the will and then packed his bag. "I'd best be going. I'm travelling."

The necessary pleasantries were said and Sam, knowing they needed to figure out this new cog in the wheel of their truce, gave him a pointed look.

"I'll see the gentleman off."

Nevada scooted closer. "Amy, I had no idea..."

A bitter smile crossed her lips and she nodded. "You deserve it more than I."

She rose swiftly.

Nevada grabbed her wrist. "Amy, wait."

She kept her back to him. "I've got nothing to say, Nevada. I hate this place. I hate ties. They imprison..."

Her voice shook. The soft scent of her perfume assailed his senses and before he could think it through, he pulled her closer. Her eyes lit with surprise. "Ties are what you make of them, Amy."

She shook her head. "I couldn't possibly hang around for three months. What do I know to do here? My life is in LA."

"Don't make any decisions right away."

She gave a bitter laugh. "My dad already made the decision. It's either I do one or the other. No middle ground."

Nevada sighed. "I get your point." He brushed a strand of hair from her face. Before he could think it through, he leaned down, brushing his lips against hers. She closed the distance between them and Nevada captured her lips.

Amy sagged against him, her hands tangling in his hair as she returned his kiss. After a moment, he broke the contact.

She closed her eyes and leaned into him. Nevada held her close. "Maybe you could call your boss."

"And say what?" Amy pushed away and dropped into the seat she'd vacated.

"Tell him what the will says."

She shook her head. "Nevada, um, this thing between us can't work."

"I get that." He ignored the flash of pain. "I mean, what would a city girl want with a horse-cattle-smelly ranch hand?"

She didn't say anything. What possessed him in the first place?

He walked out of the house. Ignoring Sam who sat on the porch swing, Nevada strode to the truck. He banged the door and cranked the ignition. Pressing down on the gas he roared out of the ranch.

He drove on for a few minutes allowing the rush of air to clear his head. He plowed his hand through his hair calling himself all manner of names. What was he thinking?

Minutes later, he drove into the parking lot of Stacy's Diner and killed the engine. His head was clearer. A number of cowboys occupied several tables. The rush hour was over and there were fewer customers. He nodded in their general direction and took a seat. He wasn't sure why he came yet.

"Nevada, it's been a while." He turned and dragged some air through his lungs summoning a smile for Stacy. "Yeah, been busy. How's work?"

"Great, what'll you have?"

"Two cups of latte, special. Where's Nina?"

"She called in sick. Be right up."

A few minutes later, steaming Styrofoam cups in both hands and a small bow to Stacy, he stepped out of the diner and into the truck.

Chapter Nineteen

Angel followed Nevada as they walked from room to room. He was buying time. After making a complete tour of the cabins, he ran out of reasons to stall.

"We've toured these buildings times without numbers, what gives?"

Nevada picked up one of the cups and handed it over to his friend.

"Talk to me, what's with the face? You're practically moping."

Nevada plunked down on the bed in the room they were in and motioned his friend to sit.

"Was the will reading that bad? I've not seen you in this state in a long while."

"It went well." At his friend's raised brow, he went on to explain. "He left the ranch to Amy quite all right but gave her a condition."

"Is that so bad? You look like you lost someone dear."

Nevada took a swig and grimaced as the hot drink scalded his tongue. His eyes stung which had less to do with the pain than the confession he was about to make.

"The condition was that she stay here for at least three months with me in charge." His gaze was intent on his drink.

"Okay," Angel drew out. "It's not such a bad idea, you know."

A sad smile tugged at his mouth, the first he had allowed since he walked out of the den. "I guess you'll tell that to Amy." He met his friend's gaze.

"She doesn't want to? Is that what she said?"

"She's made it clear she hates this place."

Angel chuckled softly.

"You think it's funny?"

"What did you say in response?"

"I kissed her," he said, making a helpless gesture. "But then she said the thing between us couldn't work."

"I didn't know the two of you had something going on."

Nevada grimaced. Restless, he stood and paced from one end of the rectangular room to the other.

Angel chuckled again, the rumble filling the room.

"Did I make a mistake telling you my tale of woe?"

Angel seemed to recover then and he came to stand beside Nevada, a hand on his shoulder.

"No, except that I'm yet to see two people who are so stubborn like the two of you." He got serious. "You should talk about it. If you meant it when you kissed her, maybe it would have made some difference."

"I meant it." The first time he was admitting in so many words that he felt something for Amy.

"Then, talk to her."

What would he do without this man? Their gazes locked for a brief moment and they shared a hug. He knew what he must do.

. . ⚘ . .

HOW COULD SHE BLAME her father for using the only means he knew to safeguard the ranch?

She was going to lose her job if she asked for three months off. That was crazy.

Dad, what were you thinking?

Alone with only her thoughts for company last night, she'd known misery in no small measure. Stay and lose her job, go, and lose the ranch. Did her dad intend to force her hand? Whatever choice she made, none would come easy.

Her thoughts strayed to Nevada. He misunderstood her, or maybe she didn't pass the message across clearly. If she chose to leave, what happened to their relationship? She liked him, a lot. She wanted to stay back, to stay with him. But her life wasn't here. And that was what she wanted to tell him. What had he said about ties? Did he mean her ties with him could be worth her while? Yeah, he was attracted to her but he never said he loved her.

Give him a break, she chided.

"Dial said to tell you to give him a call when you're ready."

Amy didn't look at Sam. "I'll be out in a bit."

The absence of footsteps proved Sam was still there. She zipped the travelling bag and dragged it off the bed to dump at her feet. After last night, she hadn't wanted to ask Nevada to drive her to the airport. Swallowing through a dry throat, she blinked.

The last twelve hours had been an eye opener for her. Going up to her father's room for the first time since she'd come home, she'd seen the pictures of generations of Jaydens' who had handed the ranch down until it reached her father. Was she going to fail her family?

Amy couldn't answer that just yet. She called Dial to inform him she was ready.

Slipping her phone away, she picked up her bag and walked over to give Sam a hug.

"You don't intend to honor your father's wish?" Amy didn't give her an answer because she wasn't sure how to go about doing that just yet. She hugged Sam closer. "I'll give you a call." And she was gone, dragging the bag behind her.

Dial took it from her and put it in the truck bed.

"Do you know where Nevada is?" she asked Dial.

"Not sure, he headed towards the back of the house," he said, pointing.

The young man seemed to squirm.

She needed to see Nevada, even if she'd end up fidgeting too but she needed to clear the air between them. "I'm sorry for keeping you from your work. I'll be right back."

She walked in the direction of the barn, careful not to draw attention until she reached him.

"You shouldn't sneak up on people like that." His voice caused the heat to burst in her and spread into her face. She had not even noticed him. She stuttered an apology, her rehearsed speech taking flight from her scrambled thoughts.

He walked out from the dark interior of the barn and then lounged nonchalantly at the door. "You needed something?" he asked, his eyebrows rose.

"Um, y-yes." She couldn't articulate her words. He didn't look hostile like she'd expected. Taking in the man before her in his cowboy boots and Wranglers, the times he'd held her because she was upset flashed before her eyes and she blushed furiously. "About yesterday. Um...I came to explain what I meant."

He stared at her, his eyes hopeful. "I...am not sure what to do just yet until I get to work. But, if I end up deciding not to come back, I'm sure you don't want..." she stammered to a halt.

The lopsided smile he gave her did nothing to ease her regrets. "I get that, Amy."

She searched his face. "It's got nothing to do with you."

"Thanks for letting me know."

She hesitated, then smiled. "I'm leaving." He only nodded, not moving from his place at the door. She should turn and let him be.

He left his place at the door and walked toward her, stopping shy of a few inches. "Can we talk?"

She hesitated briefly and then nodded. He led her to the stack of hay and gestured for her to sit. She noticed the distance he kept between them. "Before you say anything, can I ask a question?" *Salvaging her ego, huh?*

"Ask anything."

"I know I've given you a hard time since I came back, yet, you treated me well. Whatever happens from here on out, can we stay friends?"

"Yes." His response was so soft she was sure she imagined it, but it stood in his eyes.

His finger drew small circles on her hand, each causing a welling up inside her. She felt for this cowboy what she felt for no one before. But her life wasn't here.

"I'd really like to be more than a friend." He grinned. "But friendship is a good place to start."

Maybe he felt he'd said too much, because he let go of her hand and stood. She waited but he didn't say anything else.

She left the barn and walked away, without a backward glance. If she looked at him one more time, she'd be tempted to stay.

Nevada had opened his heart to her, even though he obviously held back.

Her heart was content.

Chapter Twenty

Nevada watched her walk away taking a part of him with her. His tone had come off harder than he'd have wanted because of the way his heart had reacted when he sensed her. Nevada had to rein in his defenses. He'd wanted to talk with her last night but she was nowhere to be found. Hanging around the kitchen late didn't improve his chances. Sometime around midnight he'd gone off to bed.

He'd have driven her if she'd asked but she didn't. Maybe the drive would have been awkward for both of them. Shrugging, he walked out of the barn. He couldn't even remember why he was here, and then it dawned on him that he'd come out here hoping she'd come find him.

Standing there and chewing her lip, he'd seen how vulnerable she was. If anything, he found himself tumbling deeper into whatever he'd been free falling into since he set eyes on her that first day. Another thought struck him; she had come to apologize even when she wasn't sure what his response would be.

He couldn't stay angry with her for long.

IT HAD BEEN TWO WEEKS since she left Water Hole Ranch.

Eric didn't plan to give her any more time away. How was she going to fulfil her father's wish? What would happen to everyone on the ranch if it got sold and the money given to charity?

It wasn't fair to them.

Amy reread her resignation. Not much choice otherwise. At the expiration of the three months, she'd sell off and find another job. But she owed her father, Sam, and the ranch hands that much. She was burning her proverbial bridge.

In all sincerity the city had lost its glow for her and that desire had been replaced by that for the ranch and a certain ranch hand. She'd have to earn her place at the ranch. Was he still interested in being more than her friend? It hurt a bit that in the two weeks she'd been away, he hadn't called her once.

Who says you couldn't have called too?

As she dropped her bag into the rental car, she remembered another day like this weeks ago. She'd made the same trip except that in this one, the car couldn't go fast enough.

She hardly paid attention to the scenery as she drove towards the ranch. As she neared, her breath hitched a notch higher, her belly doing flips.

She hadn't given herself an opportunity to explore what she felt about the ranch or Nevada except that she was going to give herself a chance to see if she could love the land again. Being tied to the land may not be so bad after all.

· · ❧ · ·

AMY WAS HOME. HE'D missed her. He hadn't spoken with her in the two weeks since she'd left, because he didn't want her to feel pressured. But she had occupied his every waking moment and the last thing he thought about before he dropped off to sleep.

He'd prayed for her to find happiness. Was she happy? Nevada hadn't felt such an overwhelming pull toward any woman as he felt for her—not even with Brooke and he wasn't quite sure what to do.

Maybe he'd do nothing.

Was she planning to stay? The bag she brought was much bigger than the one she came with the last time. Dared he hope?

Nevada went to the barn to feed the horses. Now that calving was over, they were down a few hands. After that, he'd go riding.

Hopefully, it would clear the web in his head. Seeing Amy probably had something to do with it.

One look at her enthusiastic smile had made his heart leap and close in its wake was the urge to hug her. She looked as though she was happy to be home.

Except that they'd greeted each other like awkward teenagers. She wanted friendship and Nevada told himself he should keep his distance from the curvy redhead whose elegant height reminded him of a gazelle and her constant blushing sent his pulse racing and his blood pressure sky high.

But how could he, when in the last two weeks it was as if she hadn't gone away, for how much she was lodged in his thoughts.

He fed the horses, whispering soft words to them. He went to Black Knight's stall. Nevada hadn't walked the horse in days. "Hey buddy boy, you up for a ride this morning?"

The horse snorted in response nuzzling the hand that rubbed between his eyes. Nevada allowed the horse to eat while he cleaned out the stalls, something to keep him occupied.

Work helped to ease his mind when he was worried about something. He shoveled and packed the dirt in the wheelbarrow, then made a trip to the spot where he emptied it for Sam's vegetable garden.

He returned back repeatedly until he'd finished cleaning.

The ranch would soon be stirring and he better got his riding out of the way before the day's chores.

He led the black horse out of the stall and came face to face with Amy. The now familiar cartwheel in his gut started but Nevada told himself sternly she was a no go. There was just that possibility she would fulfil her three months and be gone again.

"Good morning," she said, giving him a smile.

"Good morning. You're up early. "

"Yeah, I just wanted to walk around a bit." Her gaze took in the area.

His heart was hopeful. "Yes."

She returned her eyes to his. "You are doing a great job with the place."

His heart soared. He wanted her to appreciate what he saw and did with the land. "Thank you," he said, meaning it.

An awkward moment passed when they didn't seem to know what to say to each other. Amy recovered first. "Are you going riding?"

"Yes, you want to come?"

"You want company?" she asked.

"That's if you want. It's no big deal."

She chewed her lip, uncertain. The day he'd taken her riding after her dad's funeral flashed in his mind's eye. "Amy, you don't have to if you don't want to."

"I want to."

Ignoring the fluttering in his chest, he handed over the reins of *Black Knight*. "Here, hold this, let me get Spicy." He went into the barn and soon returned with another horse, a replica of the one whose reins were in her hand. "He's her sire, but they are no way alike. She's gentle. You shouldn't have any problems."

He set a saddle on the horse.

"I'll ride bareback."

"Are you sure?"

"Positive." she responded, her eyes meeting his.

He returned the saddle back to its place. "Here we go, let me help you up."

Twining his fingers together, he gave her a boost and she slid onto the horse's back. He let his hand linger briefly on her ankle.

Amy's gaze flew to his. What was she thinking? He winked at her, then walked over to the big stallion and in one fluid movement, got on its back. Silently they walked the horses at a sedate pace.

The early morning sun was just making an appearance and Nevada loved the golden paint across the sky. Its warm fingers sneaked into his jacket, dissipating the cold.

He glanced at Amy. Caught staring, she looked away, but not before her cheeks tinged with color. Did she miss him? Nevada wished this was for real—he and Amy.

• • ⚬ • •

WHAT DID THE BIBLE say about bitterness, not to let it take root? It'd crowded out everything in her life. She, who used to be adventurous and free spirited. She, who loved the little things of life and couldn't get enough of everything, didn't want to live for a while.

Moving away was supposed to have helped. But, gradually, her hatred for the land just wouldn't let up and she'd stayed away.

"Easy on the reins so you don't give her a wrong signal."

His words broke into her thoughts. "Uh, okay." She eased her hold. Longing to feel the exhilaration of riding she pointed in the opposite direction. "Look."

As he turned to see what she pointed at she nudged the horse and it took off like a flash of lightning. In split seconds, Nevada realized what she'd done.

The sound of hooves sped after her and she bent low, speaking soft words urging her horse to go faster. The breeze swept over her, combing through her hair.

She loved it.

Amy cast a quick glance behind. Nevada would catch up in no time. Laughter bubbled inside her and spilled out. Oh, laughter is medicine for the soul, she thought with a chuckle. Two Sundays in church, and she seemed to have opened a memory chest of scriptures. Mom had taught her well, and even though she'd let it go, it was for a season.

She noticed something in the distance just as Nevada caught up with her and she reined the horse to a stop. She slid off before he slowed his horse. "Let's do this again."

"I'll look forward to it but I'll be sure to give you a taste of your own medicine."

She burst out laughing and he joined in. "I can imagine how difficult it must be for you, cowboy, to be beaten by someone who hasn't been on a horse in years."

He snorted. "You cheated and we both know it. Quit preening like you won a fair competition."

Whatever it was that she'd seen earlier caught her eyes again. The land was a place for all manner of wildlife, but this didn't look like wildlife. "I see something."

"What?"

"I'm not so ... oh, a calf. How did it come so far away?"

"It walked obviously," Nevada said chuckling. "Must've wandered out and didn't know its way back."

"Oh baby, it's so cute." She walked over and knelt beside it, very aware of the man beside her. "If we hadn't come, it would have been meat for a fox or any number of predators around. You think it's ours?" The word "Ours" sounded good in her ears.

"No. The color's different. We'll take it back home and check with the neighbors."

Amy picked up the calf, held it to her chest and rose. Her gaze met Nevada's. The animal squirmed in her arms. "Hey, it's okay. You're safe." Amy stroked the neck.

"You can't carry that on the horse. It's heavy."

"I can. You could hold it for me while I climb on and then hand it over."

"Okay then."

The calf grabbed her hair and Amy had to rescue the strands from its mouth. She giggled. "Definitely not food."

She mounted Spicy and held out her hands.

Nevada placed the calf in her arms, his gaze not leaving her face. She read the surprise in his eyes. "Contrary to what you think, I haven't always hated the ranch..."

He smiled. Feeling vulnerable, she turned away. "Let's head back before Sam starts to wonder where I am."

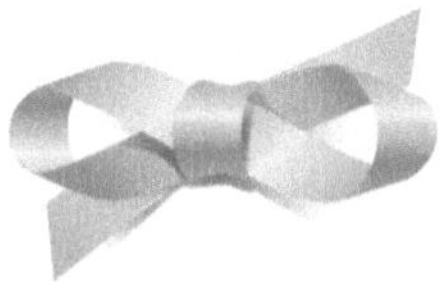

Chapter Twenty-one

He didn't respond to her. Did he dare believe that her heart was softening towards the place? In order to not raise his hope and have it dashed away, he tried to turn his thoughts from that direction.

Except that his eyes had a mind of their own because his gaze soon drifted to her.

Amy held the calf tenderly in her arms, her hair fluttering around her face. She was graceful. No one would think she'd not ridden a horse for a while, if he didn't count the one following Anthony's funeral.

He'd got a kick when she raced him down the land. Another side of her unveiled before his eyes. Carefree, her face pink from the excitement and the wind. He'd never be the same again. "You know what?"

"What?" she asked, looking at him.

"You remind me of the story Jesus told about the shepherd and his missing sheep. Even though the shepherd didn't know where his sheep was, it didn't stop him from going to look for it. A single one for him was precious and worth the trouble. Same way God treats every one of us."

She nodded.

The soft hoof-falls were rhythmic, and the gentle breeze made the morning lovely. He remembered how he'd met with the Lord and wondered if she would one day do the same, or if all she'd been through had only further alienated her from God.

"I went to church these past weeks."

"You did?" he asked, hopeful. "So?"

She smiled. "So, nothing."

The fact that she went on her own volition was something.

There were many things he was yet to know about the woman who had gradually wormed her way into his heart.

They rode back to the ranch. Nevada helped her settle the calf in a stall, bottle-feed it, and together they rubbed the horses down.

"Have you been able to raise the loan?"

"Not everything. We paid enough to stall foreclosure. With the trail ride coming soon, if we get the heads of cattle to the buyer, we'll see how much that can raise. I'm still on it. I still have a week to meet your deadline."

"I want to help you. I have some money."

He shook his head. "Not yet. Let's see what happens by the time the week is up."

"Why don't you want me to help?" She tucked her hair behind her ear.

"If we can figure this out, there's no point letting you spend money you have saved." She opened her mouth and Nevada placed a finger to her lips. "Not just yet, Amy. When I think we can't find a way, I'll let you know. Trust me."

"Promise?"

Nevada nodded.

But he liked that she was beginning to take interest in the land. In that area, she was making progress.

. . ∞ . .

TWO DAYS LATER, NEVADA scanned the sky above the flat prairie. Angry clouds gathered in the distance heralding a storm. Flashes of lightning sped across the sky.

An uneasy feeling tightened his gut.

His gaze drifted to the pens where the new calves and their mothers were held. The shelter should hold, with God on their side.

Squinting to the right he registered the ranch hands moving animals to more secure pens. It wouldn't do for the young calves to be caught in the storm or the ensuing stampede when others scampered for safety. He made his way to the horses' stalls to ensure they were bedded down without problems.

Everything was as it should be and he should have been satisfied but a niggling persisted in his mind.

His new level of relationship with Amy nagged at him. Those heart pumping smiles always had a way of melting his insides. Friendship with her was going to be hard. He wanted more. But dare he ask?

A clap of thunder caught his attention and he stepped out of the stall to study the sky again. The expanse of repair had not given him time to check the rest of the fence. *Let it hold, Lord.*

Clouds that roiled in the distant horizon had moved closer in the time he'd allowed his mind to roam unwelcomed territories. He rubbed the back of his neck, deep in thought.

Warnings of an impending storm had been going on for days but the gut feeling he could always rely on said this was no longer a warning, they were in for a real hit.

He was walking towards the pens where the others were working when he spotted Amy. The sight of her set to course a warm glow in his heart. Nevada swallowed a groan.

"Amy." He touched the brim of his Stetson and was rewarded with a broad smile that spread across her face. Her smile banished thoughts of the storm, made him forget for a spell.

She walked up to him. "I hope I'm not disturbing you?"

"No. There's a mighty storm coming."

"I hate storms."

He held her gaze. Clad in form fitting jeans, tee-shirt, and boots, she looked like she was made for the place just like she looked so right on the horse.

She raised a slender hand and pushed her hair from her face. Nevada swallowed at the unconscious gesture. The red tresses fell right back in place. For a moment, he wanted to run his hands through her hair and find out if it was as heavy and as soft as it looked. He did a quick backpedaling.

His gaze slipped to her mouth and he applied mental clamps to that line of thought, too. It would lead him nowhere. Nevada forced his gaze away and asked. "Why?"

"I had a nasty experience some years ago." She dipped her hands in her back pockets.

She wasn't willing to say so he went on. "I don't mind storms except after the calving season. Unfortunately, that's usually when they happen," he said, trying for nonchalance. He wouldn't pry into her past. Most of what he knew about her, he'd heard from Sam and their short conversations here and there.

Another slow rumble of thunder sounded and he counted silently. Before he reached twenty a flash of lightning rent the sky. It was coming faster than he thought. "I'm going to see how the cattle are settling." She fell in step with him. "Amy, you best be heading back to the house before the rain descends. I'll check on you."

She looked at him. "Uh, okay."

Was she disappointed? The rain was part of the reason he wanted her to go back, but more especially because his senses hummed at high alert. He still didn't know why she'd returned to the ranch and what the likelihood she'd stay was. If he kept his distance, he might be able to keep his head about him and what was left of his heart.

• • ❧ • •

DISTANT THUNDER RAPPED ominously. Amy cast a swift glance heavenward. The clouds were swiftly moving in to fill a third of the sky. It looked like a boiling cauldron rolling across the horizon.

The lowing of cattle and the neighing of horses came to her ears—a sure sign of restlessness. Animals were able to sense impending disaster quickly. She looked back.

Nevada had disappeared. Will he be safe?

Get a grip! She told herself sternly but that hold was fast slipping. Where went her ideology of no ties? A large drop of rain hit her arm, followed by another.

Shelving her turmoil and concern for his safety, she jogged the rest of the way. As she hit the porch, the windows of heaven opened and for a moment she wondered what the days of Noah had been like.

Knocking her boots together to remove the dirt, she entered the living room. "Hey, Sam, are you in there?" she asked peeping into the kitchen which seemed to be the woman's constant abode now that they were preparing for the trail ride.

Nevada hadn't said anything to her. She'd have to ask him about letting her go with them. A lot was changing with her and she realized it wasn't so bad.

Judging by the way dark clouds covered the sky, night would fall swiftly, a long one at that.

Rubbing her arms to ease the goosebumps, she started when a thunderclap rent the quiet. If this was LA, Mel would be there. How would Amy handle this storm? Not finding Sam, she went to her room in search.

She found the woman lying in her bed. It was unlike Sam to be resting in the middle of the day. "Are you okay?" Amy asked, alarm rising.

"I'm fine, just a tad tired."

Amy came to sit beside Sam on the bed and took her hand. Amy felt Sam's forehead. Thankfully, it wasn't warm. She couldn't imagine anything happening to Sam. She gave Amy a smile and her fear eased.

"Please be fine." Her voice sounded shaky even to her own ears.

"Are you okay?"

Amy blinked back tears. Her emotions were topsy-turvy. Amy wasn't sure if it was her worries for Sam, the storm, or her feelings for Nevada that troubled her. Especially that he seemed to want to keep her at arms-length. She was in love with Nevada but she wasn't ready to face up to that with anyone.

"Are you all right?" Sam was too perceptive.

"Silly me, I thought I'd outgrown my fear of storms." The pounding of rain and wind on the roof was unrelenting.

Sam squeezed her hand. "You know I won't mind if you come sleep here with me. I have space for two."

"I may take you up on that but rest awhile. Let me check if Nevada's back so I can lock up." She kissed Sam and stepped away.

As she walked out, she remembered Nevada no longer lived in the ranch house.

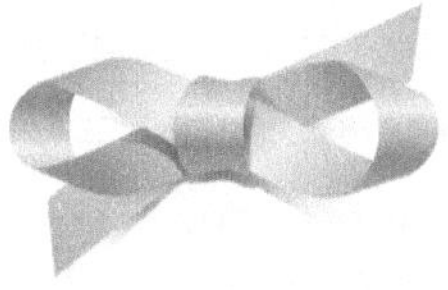

Chapter Twenty-two

Nevada bounded up the porch. His shirt and jeans were plastered to his body. He should've bunked down with the others since the bunkhouse was closer. But he had to make a stop. He needed to make sure Sam and Amy were fine. Unfortunately, he didn't have his phone.

Keep telling yourself that. Really, he could have used Angel's but he remembered Amy said she hated storms and he wanted to ... do what?

Would he babysit her? He pulled off his boots, set them away from the rain and went through the kitchen. "Where's Sam?"

"She's resting." She looked up from the book she was reading and flushed a vivid red.

He glanced down at himself. His tee-shirt stuck to his chest like plaster of Paris. "I must look a sight. Let me get out of this."

He didn't wait for a response. He had to get out before the laughter that rumbled in his chest let loose. She'd only be more embarrassed.

Ten minutes later he set his umbrella against the wall and stepped into the living room just as lightning flashed. A deafening thunder followed in its wake.

Amy dropped the mug she was holding. She jumped back as it crashed to the ground in a boom that rivaled the thunder. She cast a frightened look about her.

The lights flickered and went out.

Thankfully, Nevada had his phone on him now. He flipped on the light and came toward her. He took in the spill on the rug. "Let me get the mop."

"No!" she said, "Not yet ... please stay."

He took a few seconds to think about it, "How about you come with me? If we don't get this out on time, it will smell something awful by morning. Careful, so you don't step on the shards."

He stretched out his hand to her and she took it. Silently they padded to the closet where Sam kept cleaning supplies.

Why was Sam sleeping at this time? It was unusual, but now he had to make sure Amy was okay, then he'd check on Sam.

When they returned back, he had the place cleaned up.

The wind howled big time and he prayed the ranch would be spared from too much damage. The last time they had a huge storm, four years ago, it'd been devastating. Anthony had made improvements in the buildings since then. He hoped it helped.

Sitting on the big sofa, he patted the spot beside him. Nevada put his arm around her shoulders. If only things were different. If she were cuddled up next to him as his wife instead of...

He pictured many evenings like this one and maybe a child or two playing around. What would she look like pregnant? Nevada hid a sigh. "Tell me about your experience that's got you so scared." He turned off his light and they were plunged into darkness.

"It happened when I was twelve, so long ago, huh? There was a storm, much worse than this. Lightning and claps of thunder were incessant, booming through the air."

He sensed the tension ease from her shoulders as she spoke.

"I was in my room, but couldn't sleep. We used to have this big tree behind the house on my side of the building. I guess the tree lost a branch in all the wind and rain and crashed through the roof."

She shivered and he ran his hand gently down her arm to soothe her. After a brief moment she continued, "The roof caved in and before I could escape, a part of it ran into me and got stuck in my belly. I remember the excruciating pain and screaming but nothing after that. I guess I passed out from fear. When I came to, I was in the ER but God had mercy on me, it wasn't too deep and the damage was not much. In one week, I was out of the hospital but the memory of that day hasn't been tempered by time."

Nevada didn't know what to say, he ran his hand over her hair and then lifted a handful. Soft and light. He sighed and let it drop. "I'm glad you didn't suffer much injury."

The roof must have been changed to the pattern it now had to accommodate an apartment up in the loft. His 'upper room,' Angel called it.

"Will you stay in the house tonight?"

"You want me to?"

She nodded.

"I will."

"Thank you."

He kissed her head. "You're welcome."

Amy snuggled closer, and Nevada's breath caught. He loved Amy. God help him.

Companionable silence filled the room and Nevada listened to the storm. It seemed to be dropping in intensity.

They had been sitting in peaceful silence for about an hour when her breathing changed. She had fallen asleep.

What was God's will in all of this? Why did he feel things for her? Sometimes, like now, he'd been tempted to think there was a possibility of a future for them, other times he wasn't so sure.

She shifted and snuggled closer and he wrapped his arms around her. So innocent in her sleep.

Another half hour passed before silence descended on the land.

The storm had passed, he needed to go and see how things were.

Soft footfalls sounded down the stairs. Sam? Had she really slept through the storm? He'd never seen her sleep earlier than twelve a.m.

He eased Amy out of his arm and then picked her up. Another day some weeks ago came to mind. She'd been embarrassed and blushed furiously when she saw him the next day.

Amy was an enigma, her face very expressive of everything she felt. Sam stepped out of his way as he took her upstairs. Power came back on as he returned downstairs.

"She's always scared of storms," Sam said when he walked back into the kitchen.

"She told me."

He caught Sam's gaze and looked away, whatever was on her mind she'd say. He scouted the refrigerator for something to eat and settled on leftover pasta which he put into the microwave, and set the timer. Did Amy eat?

"I'm glad you two are getting along better."

The microwave timer went off. Nevada grabbed his meal. He'd just eat then head out. He realized he was afraid to see what damage there would be. "Me, too." He took the stool and sat opposite Sam and wolfed down his meal.

"Give her time, all right?"

He nodded, looking at Sam and then remembered he'd intended to check on her. "Are you okay? You slept through the storm."

"I'm fine and I wasn't really sleeping. I'm just tired and feeling aches in my body."

He dropped his spoon, frowning. Sam shrugged. "How long?"

"Two days, but really it's nothing."

"You need to see the doctor in the morning," When she started to protest, he shook his head, "Sam, please. We'll just make sure you're fine, is all. Have you eaten?"

"Not yet."

He took another plate, scooped some food onto it and placed it before her. What was it with these women? They didn't ever complain.

If Sam had to stay in bed then it was more than she was making out. "Eat as much as you can." He stood beside her until she started to eat then he went back to his seat.

"You know you can really be a bully."

Nevada chuckled. "When I have to. I guess I'll never understand you women."

It was Sam's turn to chuckle and then she fell silent for a moment. "You love Amy."

It was a statement but he sensed she required an answer. If he said no, he couldn't fool Sam or himself. "Uh, yeah."

"What do you plan to do about it?"

"Nothing." Finishing up his meal, he filled his cup with water from the tap and drank. He couldn't put this off forever. Taking his plate to the sink, he washed it. "I'm going out for a bit."

"Okay, don't be long."

Nevada walked into the night and detoured to the pen where the new calves were. The shelter had survived the thrashing of the storm.

"It was a mean storm, boss," Angel said as he came out of the pen, Dial at his heel. "Thank God the shelter held. The side fence we spent weeks fixing is flat on the ground, I haven't been to check the other side since it's still too dark to see far."

"How about the other cattle?" he asked, running his hand through his hair. They couldn't afford another expense.

Chapter Twenty-three

The sun was up and so bright no one would've thought there'd been a storm save the destruction it had left in its wake—a downed fence as far as the eyes could see, sheets taken from the barn roof allowed rain to soak through the hay left from winter.

The first major rain they had and then this.

Nevada inspected the stretch of fence noting in a small book the supplies they'd need to fix the expanse. It could've been worse, though. But, even at that, the new expenses would set the ranch back financially.

The trail ride was days away, and against what he'd have wished for, he'd have to use part of the money to buy the things they needed. But then, how would he pay the loan? Was he just being pig-headed in refusing Amy's help? This was her father's ranch for crying out loud. Was he willing to gamble it on the chance that he'd get the money?

He'd need to talk to her later. In the light of the new expenses, did she have enough?

I'm learning to trust You for our needs. Lord, help us out of this. And Lord I'm grateful for all You've helped me through. This is but a light thing for You.

Nevada turned in the direction where the other ranch hands dug holes for posts. They had much laid out to do and he was thankful that the fatigue of the calving season was tapering off.

"Angel, I'm heading off to town to pick up a few things. I've ordered new posts and they should arrive soon."

"Okay, we'll go on here."

· · ❧ · ·

AMY WATCHED FROM WHERE she stood at her window upstairs. She'd been thinking of how she'd get around to helping Nevada. The deadline she gave him ended in a few days and they both knew it.

In the last couple of days, she found it wasn't only his will to keep the ranch anymore. The devastation from the storm would have set him back more.

He turned from Angel and took long strides toward the truck. The moment he drove away, Amy went to the dresser and picked up a comb. She worked it swiftly through her hair, wincing as it snagged knots. Then, she changed into jeans, a blouse, and threw on a jacket. The cold front had returned since the storm.

Not sure how long Nevada would be away, she had to act fast. The new development meant she needed to take action.

Starting from today, she was getting involved in the ranch. She went into the kitchen, prepared some of Sam's coffee, grabbed some snacks from the ones Sam had been making for the trail ride and headed out. "Good morning, Angel. I brought you some refreshments."

He straightened from what he was doing and favored her with a big smile. Amy smiled back, glad that he didn't affect her the same way Nevada did.

"Thank you, my lady. It's a fine morning." He looked around, the smile not leaving his face. He wiped the sweat from his brow and took the small tray from her hand.

"Is there anything I can help you with?" Amy was beginning to question the reason for her doing this. Pushing the thought away, she waited.

"Nothing you can do, my lady."

"It's Amy. And I don't want any more "lady" here," she said laughing.

"Okay, my...."

"Not one more," she wagged her finger at him trying to act stern. He laughed and she joined in. Then he became serious.

"We could've done without the storm for now with the bank breathing down our necks."

"I'm thinking of going into town to see the bank manager tomorrow."

Angel popped a cookie in his mouth and sipped the coffee, skepticism apparent in his brown eyes that seemed to see through her. "Is it about the loan?"

"Yes. I know Nevada's been trying to raise some money but I'm sure he'll be using that to get supplies to fix the damage from the storm." Her hand swept the expanse of destruction for emphasis. "I just don't want him to owe more in order to save the ranch. Plus, he has to deal with the repairs and plan for the trail ride. Guests are due to arrive in the next couple of days."

Angel took the cup to the stump that sat beside the fence. Amy wondered if he was considering whether to say anything about his friend or not.

"Why not mention it to him? It's better that way." He returned back to the holes he'd been digging.

"I have, but he said I should hold off for now."

Angel finished his digging and dragged a pole into it. He secured the pole and then turned to her. "Why are you helping now when you've been all for selling?"

"I don't know exactly. My memories of this place are bad and I haven't forgotten them." She licked suddenly dry lips. "I've seen Nevada's love for the land and I'm beginning to love it too."

There was a brief silence. Two other ranch hands who worked a distance away cast occasional glances at them.

"Nevada used up his savings."

Amy frowned. "Are you serious?"

"Yup."

It would be cruel of her to sell the land he'd given his all for. It also changed her opinion about him. He was one to go all the way out. Saving the ranch was both theirs to pursue even if they didn't agree on how best to do it.

She'd been rash in issuing a deadline. She would rectify that tomorrow. She stepped in beside Angel and grabbed a hammer and some nails.

A heavy sigh escaped her as memories of her with her dad so long ago flashed in her mind. Missing her mark, she hit her hand. Amy swallowed a whimper and went on with the work.

She'd feel the pain at the end of the day but her dad would be proud. If only he could see her now. It more than made up for her throbbing thumb.

"I'm sorry dad," she whispered.

. . ❧ . .

WAS THAT AMY? NEVADA turned into the driveway and cut the engine. It was her all right. The sun caught on her red hair pulled back in a ponytail.

What was she doing? *Working, dummy,* a small voice said.

Without gloves? How long had she been doing this?

Angel said something to her and her laughter carried on the wind across the field to reach him. His heart took a tumble. He needed to talk to her about the loan because the purchase he made for repairs had made a dent in the money he was putting together.

He felt like a failure.

Nevada climbed down from the truck grabbing the nails and wires for the fence from the truck bed. His phone rang, he checked the caller. Angel's dad. Pulse racing wildly, he accepted the call. This was his last shot.

"Hello, sir."

"Son, I'm sorry, my friend disappointed me at the last minute."

"I understand."

"I'm still waiting on one, though. But I've been feeling in my spirit that you're having so many struggles. I'm praying for you, son. Trust in the Lord with all your heart and lean not to your own understanding, in all your ways acknowledge Him and He shall direct your path."

"Thanks for reminding me, sir, I needed that." When the call ended, he slipped the phone away. What to do now?

He walked the rest of the way to reach Amy and his friend. "Amy you shouldn't be working without gloves."

"Why?" She glanced down the line of ranch hands. "They're all working without protection."

Her eyes glowed, her face flushed. Was she enjoying it? "Most of us have worked on ranches all our lives, our hands don't even feel anything, but you haven't done this."

She looked at her hands and grimaced.

"Let me see." She held them behind her and he guessed they wouldn't be good to look at. He didn't want her getting injured. He dropped the supplies on the ground. "Amy, I'll look at them one way or another and I'm sure you won't want to feed the gossip of your employees."

She bit her lip, considering, and his heart stirred. She'd been so hard at work one would think that she'd done it all her life. She held out her hands and he walked closer to take a look.

He was aware that Angel watched them. "Whoa, what's this?"

She snatched one hand back and he held fast to the other. Blisters covered the base of her left thumb and there was a moderate swelling. "You hit yourself?"

She nodded, "It's no big deal."

"It is, and I think you've done enough for one day." He rubbed gently on her palm. "Trust me, Amy. You'll feel every bit of these blisters later."

"I just want to help."

She looked like a child, eager to please. Nevada was glad they had company. Though Angel pretended to ignore them completely, his friend heard them.

He let go of her hand. "Pass the things we need, is that okay?"

"Okay then, let me get you coffee. I'll be back."

He knew Amy. The fact that she capitulated easily meant one thing, she was feeling the presence of the blisters even though she wasn't letting on. When she was gone far enough not to hear, he picked up a post and dragged it into a hole. "Why did you allow her to do this? It's not a woman's job."

He ignored Angel's knowing smile.

"I couldn't dissuade her."

"You could have."

"You'd best hold your opinion because I'm sure she won't appreciate you treating her like a child."

"This isn't about treating her like a child, you of all people know better..." he said heatedly.

"Nevada, you wear your feelings on your sleeve where Amy's concerned."

Yet, she didn't know, he wanted to say.

He would have said more, but the moment he opened his mouth, Angel coughed.

Feigning seriousness, Nevada went back to his work.

"Here you are."

Nevada took the mug and plate of cookies. "Thank you."

"Enjoy. I need to get something for the others."

She switched the thermos she slung over her shoulder and headed towards the others along the fence.

Watching her walk away, Nevada sighed. There was no going back now. She'd fully and completely captured his heart. He'd underestimated her with every turn of events. If she was any other person she'd be whining about her hand, rather she was serving others.

"Get back to work, friend," Angel said laughing. Caught red handed, Nevada laughed too.

Could he convince her to give them a chance?

Chapter Twenty-four

Amy took note of the surprise on the faces of the ranch hands as she poured them coffee. There was always a first time, right?

She smiled at one then another and then headed back. Her phone rang. Her boss's name came on the screen. Pursing her lips, she cast a quick glance at Nevada and stepped away. She didn't want him to know she quit her job. Not yet.

She was tempted to ignore the call but that wouldn't solve anything. Suppose there was something she forgot to hand over?

Swiping the screen, she put the phone to her ear. "Good afternoon, sir."

"Amy, we're having a bit of a crisis here," he said without preamble. "I'm wondering if you will consider coming back."

"I don't know, sir."

"Cut the *sir* thing. I need your help. Even if all you do is come in once every two weeks, for some time."

She sighed. Was he playing a dirty trick on her? "I'll have to think about it."

"Give me a call later, okay?"

"Sure." She dropped the phone in her pocket and looked up. Her eyes met Nevada's. How much had he overheard? "It's my boss." She picked up the mugs and set them on the tray.

"Are you having trouble with him?"

"Not really. He wants me back at work."

She saw something cross his face and was gone instantly. Was it regret? Or was he glad she was leaving? Not in the mood to work anymore, she grabbed the tray and headed toward the house.

. . ❧ . .

LATER THAT DAY, AS Amy sat at the table her phone vibrated. Eric. She should return his call but what would she tell him? For someone who wouldn't give her time off, understandably, she'd taken her only option. Amy turned the phone upside down.

"How's your hand?"

She spread out her palms and looked at them. "Fine I guess."

Nevada nodded and started to eat. Sam joined them at the table and they ate in silence. "I may have to go back to work by the weekend and come back again."

"Is your boss giving you a hard time?" Sam asked.

"No."

"I think it's high time you quit that job and come back. You can't possibly keep going back and forth," Sam said.

Nevada looked at Amy. If she told them she officially quit, what would they think? Suppose at the end of three months, she decided she really wanted her old life? Her boss was offering her an olive branch.

"I can imagine your struggle. Five years you've lived in the city and enjoyed all the good things that go along with that kind of life. Here, you'd have nothing but cattle and manure to deal with. I wouldn't blame you if you chose to return."

Did he have to be so understanding? Her father's request was something nobody talked about.

"What day would you leave?" he asked.

"Maybe Saturday if I can book a flight, so I'll be there on Monday."

"I was hoping you'd go with us for the trail ride."

"I wish I could, but I need to go back. Thanks for asking."

She gave him what she hoped was a genuine smile. He returned it and her heart stuttered. He reached out and squeezed her hand.

"Decide what you want and don't let the man toss you around," Sam said matter-of-factly.

Amy stood, took her dish and Sam's, and put them in the sink. She sliced some apple pie and put them on three plates.

"Here, let me help you," Nevada said, taking two plates from her.

They ate and talked about her work and a number of other things. Between him and Amy, they did the dishes.

"Would you like some juice?"

"Yes, thank you."

"I'll meet you on the porch."

"You want some, Sam?"

"No, I'm getting these old bones to bed. Make sure you lock up."

Amy gave her a hug. "Sleep tight."

Sam hugged Nevada and went upstairs.

They sat on the glider and allowed it to rock back and forth.

"I'm a bit worried about Sam. She's been sleeping a lot lately. The doctor gave her some medications and has asked her to take it easy for a while."

"She told me. How would you get everything ready for the trail ride? I know she's baked quite a lot but she was supposed to go with you, I guess?"

"Yes," he sipped his juice, his eyes taking in the inky black of the night sky. "The ranch cook would have to do. I only hope the guests won't be disappointed. It wouldn't hurt to tell them early what they'd be getting but we'll find a way around that." Nevada drained his juice and stood. "I have a few things to do before I turn in. See you in the morning."

Amy stood too and picked up her cup. "I'll keep yours."

He hesitated a bit and disappeared into the night. Amy rubbed the back of her neck, heaving a sigh. She hated it when he withdrew even though he apparently had something on his mind.

Amy walked into the house, plans forming in her mind.

Nevada would work himself to death to fix that fence, and she was going to help him. She dumped the cups and bounded up the stairs.

Hopefully she'd still catch Sam awake.

• • ❧ • •

AS DAWN PEEKED OUT in the sky, Nevada took his place at the fence and started to work. He didn't know how they'd be able to fix it all before Friday.

A truck turned into the driveway. Doyle and two other men climbed out. Nevada hadn't met the other two before. They walked toward Nevada, their work tools in their hands.

One of the men gave a musical yowl and said to Doyle and the other man, "To the rescue we have come, haven't we?"

"You got it," Doyle winked.

Nevada looked from one to another, shaking their hands.

"We got a call that you needed some rescuing. I'm Jake. My ranch is south of Doyle."

"Who called you?" Nevada's mind ran the possibilities.

"That's our secret. Let's get to work."

Another truck turned in—a neighboring rancher and yet another person. With the extra five people joining the ranch hands, the work got under way.

"I guess someone is really concerned about you," Angel said, coming to stand beside Nevada.

Nevada took a good look at his friend. Humor lit his eyes. Doyle had also refused to volunteer information as to who had called them. "Are you saying you didn't call them?"

"Now, why would you think I did?"

Nevada shrugged. "The work is much. Maybe you got scared that we'd age doing it."

A smile played on Nevada's lips. He really could smile, with the burden lifted. He looked at the fence, barely two hours and they had covered close to half the repairs.

The place of help couldn't be underestimated. Without it they'd be nowhere. *God, is that what You're teaching me?* "If you didn't, who did?" he asked, his gaze coming to rest on his friend.

"I'm not exactly sure, just a guess."

Angel propped his hammer on a post and walked up to Nevada, a hand on his shoulder. "I think Amy may have made the call. Stop being pig-headed and let her help you. You have worked hard to keep the ranch going. Maybe God wants you to learn to allow people to help you."

"Come on over," Sam's clear voice rang out, preventing him from answering.

Angel's hand dropped from his shoulder. Their eyes met and held briefly. "Think about it, my friend."

They turned and walked up to the others who had gathered under the shade of the barn. In another couple of hours, the repairs would be complete.

He hadn't seen Amy all day and she had not shown up at all since they started work. Maybe she'd gone out? That would be the first since she returned. Plus, only one truck sat in the driveway. He missed the fact that she hadn't come to stay with them today. But when had she made the calls? Questions chased each other across his mind.

"Thanks," he said, accepting his drink.

"You seem lost," Sam said and winked at him.

He sidestepped her elbow and laughed. She looked better today. *God, I've got reasons to thank You. Sam looks better today and You have raised us help. Thanks, God.*

He sipped his juice and listened to the jokes around him, his mind on Amy. He'd chickened out of talking with her last night, but he couldn't put it off indefinitely. Once the work was done today, he'd have free time to sort the guest list and fine tune his plans.

He had two days and the lines were beginning to fall in place. Minus the loan. Angel's words came back to him. He and Amy would talk tonight.

Chapter Twenty-five

Mission accomplished. Amy shook hands with the older man. "Thank you so much. I appreciate what you have done for us."

"It's no problem at all. Nevada is an impressive young man and I was happy to help. Your father and I have also gone way back."

She picked up her bag and Ray, the bank manager, walked her to the door. She climbed into the truck and grabbed her phone. She pulled up Eric's number. Amy's finger hovered over her boss's name for a few seconds, then she hit the dial.

"Thanks for calling, Amy."

Amy closed her eyes and wet her lips. "I'm sorry, sir. I don't think I will be able to make it."

"Why, Amy? Your replacement is a nightmare..."

"I don't know. Problem is, I have some things I need to sort out here."

"I'll pay for your trip every time you come."

"That's kind of you but I'll have to decline. I'm sorry."

The phone went dead in her ear. Great.

She relaxed and closed her eyes. She could breathe easy. It was as though a weight had been lifted from her shoulders.

· · ⌘ · ·

THE STARS TWINKLED breaking the dark. The temperature had dropped again. Looked like winter was determined to hang around for longer. "What changed?" Nevada asked.

"About what?"

He stepped down settling on the glider beside her, passed her a mug of hot chocolate, and set the glider in motion like always.

"Thank you."

"You got people to help with the fence, people you didn't really know, except Doyle, who you met a few times at the service. So, I'm wondering what changed."

"You needed help."

He slowed the motion of the glider and turned to look at her. A strand of hair brushed her smooth cheeks. Nevada reached out and tucked it behind her ear. His fingers stroked her hair briefly and then he dropped his hand. He loved this woman and she was doing things that made his fall faster and deeper. "Yeah, I needed help but weeks ago you wouldn't have done what you just did. I mean, you offered to help a few days back but, I thought …"

She took a long drink of her chocolate and he knew she was thinking through her answer.

"I'm not exactly sure," she said, turning her mug round and round. "I haven't analyzed it." She gave a small shrug and then turned a full smile on him. "I thought you'd at least be thankful instead of quizzing me. I'm sure that's not how you were taught."

"No, you bet." Nevada drained his mug and set it on the ground beside him. He reached out and took hers. She was yet to finish up and he set it beside his empty cup. She stared wide-eyed at him. "Don't be afraid, sweet. You want to know how I was taught."

She lifted her hands in surrender and laughed. "I don't want to know anymore." There was a little tremor to her laughter.

"I'd be disappointed then," he said, grabbing her hand and tugging her to him.

"Nevada, a simple thank you isn't so difficult to say." He felt the current zip through him. She must have felt it too. The laughter died in her throat as she stared at him.

Nevada cupped the back of her head and seeing her eyelids droop was all the encouragement he needed. He brought his mouth down on hers and kissed her.

He poured his feelings into that brief kiss and released her. "Thank you, Amy."

· · ❧ · ·

HIS VOICE WAS HUSKY. She reached out and ran a hand across his face. He turned her hand and pressed a kiss in her palm not letting go. Her heart stirred. If she told him she loved him and that was part of the reason she was helping, would he believe her?

He still had difficulty communicating in so many words, but he was a good listener and she could talk enough for both of them.

Things had changed between them. But, was it sufficient to think his kisses meant anything to him? She spared him a quick glance. He was looking at her. She blushed and lowered her gaze. He chucked her on the chin and drew her into his arms. It felt so right.

The night of the storm came to her. He'd been attentive and caring.

Her father had seen something in Nevada which she hadn't seen. Quick tears sprang to her eyes and she blinked them away choosing to listen to the quiet beat of Nevada's heart against her cheek instead of thinking about her loss.

After that day the will had been read, he hadn't kissed her again. Did he love her? She wanted to ask.

Her face heated. That would be the day. What was wrong with her going all mushy over a guy? How Mel would laugh. She'd been so sure this would happen.

"I'll miss you when you go. I really wish you'd come with us for this ride. It would be just a few days."

"I'm thinking about it."

When she called Mel to tell her about Eric's proposal, she'd reiterated what he'd said about the replacement and Amy had felt pity for him.

Her inability to make up her mind just yet was the reason she didn't want anyone to know that she was jobless.

Mel had jokingly told her to not bother, that Eric would sort himself out, encouraging her to stay with Nevada. She had vehemently denied that she was developing feelings for 'her cowboy' as Mel called him. Mel had said it was because Amy didn't want her to say "I told you so."

Truly, did she want to go back to the dreary-lonely-old life? Why did she ever think it was wonderful? He ran his hand over her hair and she came back to reality. Nevada was who she wanted to stay with and life on the ranch was better than her own sterile apartment in L.A.

"Don't pay me any mind. I know your job's on the line. I shouldn't be asking you...."

Amy pushed away, she needed to be sure the risk she was thinking of taking was worth it. "You really want me to come?"

His look was incredulous. His lips tipped in a smile. "I want you to come more than anything, except that you may not like it. Besides, I don't want you to lose your job on account of that."

"I'll come then."

"What about your job?" he asked, searching her face.

"I'll worry about that later."

"I know you'd be good at anything but suppose your boss lets you go? What will you do then?"

"You'd hire me."

He chuckled and then became serious. "You'll hate it in one week and you're my boss. Have you forgotten? I can't possibly hire my own boss."

"More like a boss with a condition." They both burst out laughing. "I guess my father knows me too well. I'm beginning to love the place again but I wouldn't have been around long enough to see because I'd have sold out the very next minute."

Nevada reached out and threaded his fingers through hers. "Thank you for holding off."

Amy nodded, too swamped with emotion to respond. She would give anything for her father to know that she'd decided to keep the ranch.

They stared into the night. Stars twinkled in the inky blackness of the sky, a gentle breeze blowing around them.

"I better turn in. I have a few calls to make and I need to update the logbooks." He kissed her on the top of her head and pulled her off the glider with him.

"You should consider using a computer system. It'd be easier that way."

"I know, maybe when we can afford it." He saw her to the door and then headed off towards the den.

Still neither of them had brought up the loan.

· · ❧ · ·

NEVADA STEPPED QUIETLY through the door. Amy's pulse raced at the sight of him. Except that he wasn't looking too friendly right now. "Why didn't you tell me?"

"Tell you what?" she asked.

Pretending not to know would only buy her time but not help her escape answering. "You know exactly what I'm talking about, Amy." His tone was gentle.

Why hadn't she sworn the man to secrecy? "I wanted to tell you. The time just wasn't right. I feel for the land..." *And for you.* "What I haven't felt in a long time, can't you see?" She willed him to understand.

He dropped into the opposite chair and held her gaze. "I'd been meaning to talk to you about your offer to pay the loan. And then the storm came and I wasn't sure you had enough to cover the loan."

"At one point it was only you wanting to save the ranch." She took his hand. "Don't you see two are better than one, even God says so. I saved up some money in the last five years."

He turned away and plowed a hand through his hair and then turned back to her, "Amy," a heavy sigh escaped him and all his emotions were packed in that one word, "I'm sorry, can you forgive me? I feel like I've failed you."

"Oh, come on. You haven't." She gazed into his eyes. Would he trust her enough to tell her why he felt so strongly he had to save the ranch alone? She smiled at him, "I forgive you, Nevada. How did you find out?"

"Angel's father was able to raise some money among his friends. So, I went to pay off what was left. The manager looked surprised and I couldn't fathom it. It was then he told me you'd come by yesterday to pay. That was why you were not around all morning?"

"Yes."

"You should have told me."

She gestured between the two of them. "You know you'd have refused had I told you."

"I'd been so afraid Jayden's legacy would die with you. Your dad would be proud." He came around the table and hugged her briefly. "If we didn't already have guests set up, the trail ride wouldn't be necessary. By the time we wean the calves, we should be back on track. But it could be fun, you know."

"I don't want you to cancel. I hope to experience a trail ride once."

"Did you tell your boss you weren't returning yet?"

She flushed. "Yes."

Her phone rang. "Mel," she said, winking at him.

Chapter Twenty-six

Nevada watched her as she accepted the call. He turned to the window and stared at the cabins. They were expecting five guests, a couple and three others and they'd be arriving any moment. Trying not to eavesdrop he turned his heart to the Lord.

I'm sorry Lord. Have I not been the one whining about needing help yet I hadn't recognized Your provision for me. Thank You Lord for showing me that You hear prayers. I have seen it.

Amy giggled behind him.

Lord what's in Your plan for me and Amy? I do love her but I can't even ask her to marry me with nothing to offer. Sometimes I'm not sure if she feels anything for me and I couldn't ask her for fear she'd reject me. If there's nothing in it, make Your plans clear.

"I think I should tell you something."

Nevada came back to the present. Amy's cheeks were pink. He inclined his head. "What is it?"

"Um," she rubbed her hands together. "Actually, I quit my job before I came back. I haven't told you because I was thinking I could go back. Eric wants me back but I don't want to go."

Nevada folded his arms across his chest, trying to process what he was hearing. Amy would hate the ranch in a week, he was sure of that. The isolation got to people quickly. She'd go stir crazy and what next?

"Stop looking at me as though I've sprouted horns. What do you say? I want to work with you here."

Helpless, he held her by the arms and guided her to the chair, taking a perch on the table. He touched his chest. "Amy I would be happy to have you around on the ranch but staying forever?" He tilted her chin so she'd be looking straight at him. "You'd hate it. You are not cut out for this kind of life."

He took her hands and spread out her palms for her to see. The blisters had dried but their marks were still there. He rubbed his finger across them and marveled at their softness. "I think you should go back."

She stood up and cupped his face. Nevada felt a weakness take him and he closed his eyes. He'd hate to see her come to dislike the land again and pine for what she'd lost. Would she blame him then?

"Nevada, look at me."

Her voice was pleading. He opened his eyes. "If you don't want me around, I'll go. I can go back to the city, pick up where I left off."

He inhaled her perfume and it permeated his senses. If he wasn't selfish, he'd tell her to go. Yet if he let her go now, would she understand it's because he wanted her to be happy?

Pain zipped through him and he couldn't look at her. Sighing, he dropped his gaze.

"Nevada, don't dare turn away from me. Tell me here and now, do you want me to stay or go?"

He just stared, she took her hands away and he felt a chill come on his face. He watched as she dropped into the chair again, "I'll go then."

"You don't understand."

"Then make me, Nevada. Make me understand."

"Alright, I want you to stay. But I hope you won't end up hating it all and blame me for asking this of you."

A big smile spread across her face and he wanted to keep the moment frozen in time. "I won't, you'll see."

The sound of a car came to their ears, their guests were arriving. "We better get out there."

God be with us. He prayed as he followed her out.

. . ⁂ . .

WITH EVERYONE FITTED to horses, they were ready to set out. The luggage had been piled in the chuck wagon that also carried their supplies. Nevada placed the three ice chests last. Sam sat in the truck with the supplies. Thank God, the doctor said she caught a stomach bug. "Are you sure you want to do this?"

"Very sure, go take care of things. We'll get to the lodge ahead of you and have something ready in time for a late lunch."

He gave her a quick kiss. "Thank you."

He'd resigned himself to having to eat cook's concoctions but Sam wouldn't hear of it as long as they had guests with them.

Anyway, if she wasn't looking better, he'd have refused.

Turning away he checked with his guests. "Mr. and Mrs. Rudolph, are you ready?"

"Yup." The enthusiastic smile the young wife gave him made him wish he was the man and she Amy.

He checked with the others and finally turned to Amy. He'd avoided looking at her, guilt holding him captive. She may have lost her job because he'd selfishly asked her to come. He searched her face. Was she regretting her decision? He hoped not. "Are you doing okay?"

"Yeah."

Her cheeks were flushed with color. He wanted to tell her she had nothing to fear, work or no. He wanted to kiss her. But they weren't alone.

Patting her horse, he smiled at her. "Just go easy on the reins, you'll do okay."

He walked towards the big stallion.

"Boss, we are good to go," Angel said as he, Daniel, Dial, and Diam rode toward him.

Nevada gave them instructions and then walked over to his horse. The sound of a car drew his attention to the road. A red sports car came into view, the sound of the exhaust filling the early morning air. Maybe Amy had a visitor.

He tried to ignore the disappointment that clenched his gut.

Of course, she wouldn't be going on this ride. Worse still she would've lost her job for nothing. He was hoping he could make the ride enjoyable for her so that it would make up for everything.

Could it?

The car roared to a stop close to where they stood causing the horses to shy away. The stallion stood his ground. He was better trained than the others to handle sound. His gaze flickered to Amy's and she looked askance. So, she didn't know the car.

The driver's door opened and he sucked in his breath. "Brooke."

The word escaped him before he could think. She stepped out and cast a smile in the general direction of everyone.

Her red hair flowed past her shoulders and he remembered that day, just weeks ago, when he had awoken to Amy standing over him, her hair down her back like this.

Now, he was sure Amy's was a shade darker. Brooke sashayed towards him and Nevada swallowed hard.

Lovely as ever, he'd once thought beauty equated love.

No, he wasn't going that way. He wouldn't think of what would've been because it was all in the past.

She gave Amy one cursory glance and practically dismissed her. Anger surged through him. What was she looking for after six months?

"Oh, darling," she said, draping her hand over his shoulder. She gave him a hard kiss on his cheek. "How are you?"

All eyes were on them. How would Amy feel thinking he'd invited Brooke after making her lose her own job? He took Brooke's hand off him. "What are you doing here?" he asked through clenched teeth.

She pouted and tried to link her hand through his. "Is that any way to greet your fiancée?"

"Brooke, don't make a scene here. I have guests and...."

"Yeah, I heard about your trail ride. I just invited myself along."

"This isn't some pleasure ride Brooke, so I'll..."

She snorted. "I don't see how you tell me that and she gets to fol-low."

She said pointing to Amy without sparing her a glance. Trust Brooke to be petty when she felt like it. He frowned. Amy wasn't the only female around, why was Brooke pointing to her?

"Let the young lady come along, the more the merrier," the middle-aged man named Greg said. "Or what do you think?" he asked others.

There was a general consensus and rather than make a scene, Nevada agreed to allow her to come. But he would be sure to confront her as soon as they were back.

People were easily carried away by her pretty, innocent look but all that was just skin deep.

Outnumbered, he instructed Dial to get another horse for her.

"Let's get together," Nevada said and waited for everyone to come close. "Welcome to our first spring round up." He looked around the small group. "I hope we'll be able to make this a twice a year event—spring and summer. Since this is our maiden ride, we'll use it as our baseline for other rides. Take note of what we do right and wrong. At the end of the ride, I'll want to hear your feedback, suggestions. I'll always be glad to have you back with subsequent improvement in our services to you."

He gave them a broad smile, feeling the excitement of this pet pro-ject. "This is going to be low key but, not to worry. Sam will whip up every dish imaginable for you."

The riders rewarded him with smiles.

He'd prayed about this and trusted God to help him make it worth-while for them. "We will be driving a number of cattle to the place where the buyer will pick them up. There are about fifty."

He continued. "We will be in groups of three except for the Rudolph's group where there will be four of them to afford them a little window for bird watching as they indicated interest. I hope we can accommodate that fully in subsequent rides. But maybe warmer months would be better as even the birds tend to run away from the cold."

That earned a chuckle.

"Everyone game?"

Heads nodded in agreement. "Either Angel or I will be here in case there's a problem or you need anything. Life on the ride will be like it was in the old west and we're here to make sure you enjoy your stay. We'll have one camp out in the open, and we've made provisions for the cold night or in case of rain. The first camp is about ten miles from here and you also get to sleep in a log house tonight. Does anyone have any questions?"

He looked at everyone. They shook their heads. "Good, let's set out."

All through the exchange, he hadn't dared to look at Amy. He didn't have to. He felt her presence with every fiber of his being. How did one explain about an ex-fiancée who showed up from nowhere? He hadn't heard from her since they broke up. How did she know about the ride, anyway?

He dropped back to wait for Amy who had chosen to bring up the rear. "Are you okay?"

"Yeah, I am."

He nodded. The early morning sun was just rising, warm and nice for an early ride. They'd get to the lodge before sundown. That should take them at least eight hours, with time in between for a brief rest. "I didn't invite her."

She shrugged.

He waited. "Amy, say something."

"Like what? I heard her say she invited herself. No big deal. I was just surprised that you have a fiancée."

"An ex-girlfriend, Amy. We didn't get that far before things went south. I've not seen or heard from her in months."

She nodded again, her lips pursed "But obviously she knew how to find you, what you were up to."

"Nevada, this is lovely," Brooke said.

The laughter that used to excite him grated on the nerve that was on its way to getting frayed. She rode back and planted herself between them. His opportunity to explain to Amy was lost.

Maybe their friendship, too.

Thanks to Brooke.

Chapter Twenty-seven

Amy shook her head. She shouldn't be jealous. She, who was all against being tied down, was feeling envious over a man. Ridiculous.

Not wanting to hear what the young woman had to say, Amy drew further back from them. She had no hold over Nevada whatsoever. And she couldn't complain about anything. If they were married then maybe she could be upset, but Nevada was just a regular guy.

Yet, it hurt and her eyes stung.

Why had she agreed to come? She'd never been an impulsive person but in the last few weeks she'd done a lot of on-the-spur-of-the-moment things to last the world over.

She glanced at them. When Nevada looked at her, she averted her gaze. They looked good together. The knife twisted inside her. Closing her eyes, she turned her face to the early morning sun.

"Are you okay?" Angel's voice broke into her thoughts.

She wanted to scream at him. Why did they ask? Couldn't they see she wasn't fine?

Was it so painful to be in love?

Schooling her features, she pushed her hair from her face and smiled at him. "I'm fine."

"Really?" he asked, his head inclined.

Amy wrapped the reins on her hand, careful not to shorten the length. Tears tickled the back of her throat. Maybe she should have gone with Sam and she'd not have seen this. A number of emotions crashed through her heart, her job she'd given up, then this young lady with red hair. Brooke's was finer not unruly like Amy's. She blinked and turned her eyes away. "Maybe I'm not," she said in a whisper.

"It's not what you think, Amy."

She'd come to develop a liking and respect for Angel. "She said she's his fiancée."

"What did Nevada say?"

"He said she's his ex. I know I don't have any hold on him. It's just ridiculous that I feel..." She shrugged and left the word hanging.

"Amy, trust him. It's as he says. I've known Nevada for a while and he isn't untrue to you."

She looked at him then, grateful that he was trying to make her feel better. "Thank you."

"You're welcome. Nevada is not going to let her make a scene and I'm sure he'll explain to you in time." He reached out and squeezed her hand. They continued in silence.

The Rudolphs' were bird watching. The young wife took snapshots and passed the camera to her husband. They laughed easily, like the others were not there.

Amy's heart twisted. She'd never allowed herself to consider any relationship and had guarded her heart 'with all diligence.'

When did all that change?

It was that first day she'd set eyes on Nevada. Dressed in faded denims, buttoned up shirt rolled up to the elbow and a cowboy's hat and boots, she'd known she'd have a hard time keeping her heart no matter how diligent.

Was it not better when she had nothing to worry about?

Her back was beginning to ache.

Impulse.

That was what it did to people. She hadn't ridden for long distances in a long time and she'd decided to do a trail trip.

She tucked strands of hair behind her ear then unwound the strap of the bottle on her saddle horn. Amy took a deep drink, wiped the trickle from her chin and replaced it.

The sun was getting hotter, which was the first in days.

Amy pulled her wide brim hat from her knapsack. It was extra protection anyway with the sunscreen she'd put on. She didn't need any sunburn.

Amy glanced at Nevada and Brooke. She was practically glued to his side like some besotted puppy. She did the talking and Nevada rode straight-back beside her.

Welcome to the club.

By the end of the first few miles, Amy allowed the gentle movement of the horse to sooth her misgivings. She didn't need to have him around to enjoy the trip. The ride would be what she made of it.

The sun warmed her back making her feel languid. She let her gaze roam at the beauty of the terrain God had made. Amy smiled to herself. She was beginning to think about God more.

As she succumbed to the mesmerizing sway of the animal under her, she made up her mind not to let anything mar her enjoyment of the ride.

She had her eyes open when she agreed to this ride. She'd lost her job for good by choice. Nevada had asked, yet, it was her decision to make. Humming *Amazing Grace* to herself, she gave in to the environment.

• • ❧ • •

"YOU ARE TOO UPTIGHT, Nevada," Brooke said. Her laughter was like a tinkling bell that bruised his nerves that felt like they had been strummed.

He shook his head. What was she up to? "I don't get it, why did you come? Going by the kind of car you're driving, I guess your rich boyfriend is still hanging on your arm. Or have you dumped him too?" Nevada didn't bother to hide his sarcasm.

He spared her a brief glance. She was beautiful and at one time he'd been taken by her. He was glad she didn't have a hold on him anymore.

She wasn't laughing now. "Maybe I missed you?"

Nevada couldn't help chuckling. "Brooke, feed me another line. Do you know what you're talking about at all?"

"Nevada, I'm sorry...."

Nevada raised his hand to stop her, "Don't even go there. It's been how many months?" he asked, a slow burn starting in the pit of his stomach. He shouldn't let her set him on the path of anger again.

"Time changes everything."

"Whoa. Does that mean I've stopped being a loser? Has that changed too? I'm glad you realize time changes things."

"I regret all that I said back then."

"And it took you so long to realize that, I guess? Do you take me for a fool?"

"No, I didn't know if you would want to see me."

"That's rich. I'm flattered."

"You are not normally cynical."

"Then, welcome to the new normal." He gave her a tight smile.

Why was he having this discussion with her? He glanced at the other riders. Everyone was preoccupied. Amy was by herself.

This wasn't what he had in mind for her. He felt worse, more because he'd let her put her job on the line for the ride and now this was what she got from trusting him.

He could ignore Brooke if it was just the three of them but amidst these people, it wouldn't do to start something that'd stir up gossip.

"Do we have another chance? I'll make it up to you."

"Not in this lifetime and I hope you can lay that dream of yours to rest. And I beg you, please, let this couple of days pass without a scene. I wouldn't want to embarrass you. So, I'm giving you a fair warning."

"Is it because of her?" She snorted.

Nevada nudged his horse close to Brooke. He needed to set her straight once and for all. "She is the reason I said I wouldn't want to embarrass you. If you can't be civil with her, give her a wide berth. If you push me you won't like what I'll do."

"You love her that much?"

"I don't think I'm answerable to you as to whom I love or don't." He gave her one last glance and turned to see to his guests. "You doing okay?" he asked as he fell in beside the Rudolphs.

"Yeah, right hon?" he asked, turning to his wife.

She rewarded him with a shy giggle. "You can see for yourself. It couldn't be better, even though there are fewer birds to see. I love the opportunity all the same. You should really consider doing a lot more bird watching rides for people like us."

"Would people want to do that so much?"

"Don't you know bird watching is becoming a favorite pastime for a lot of people?" Mrs. Rudolph raised her binoculars to watch an ibis perched on a tree branch.

"Would you have preferred that this was more bird watching than cattle roundup?" Nevada asked. Inside, he was seething at Brooke for showing up in the first place.

"No, I get to do both side by side so no problems there at all. There's an opportunity to see a wide range of species up close."

Nevada nodded. He'd thought of experimenting with this ride to see what they'd need for a summer one. Anyway, he'd take note of that. He listened to their discussion about birds and was impressed about the woman's intelligence.

Nevada waited to allow Greg to catch up. Talks of politics and the forthcoming election went back and forth for a few minutes. After another mile, they arrived at the pasture where the yearlings waited to be led.

Nevada rode to the chuck wagon and asked Sam to pass him drinks from the ice chest which he loaded into his knapsack. He signaled the riders to come closer. "Do you mind a little rest so that you can view the terrain better? We can herd the cattle when we are ready to leave."

There was a positive response and they stopped under a large tree. Nevada passed around chilled bottles of soft drinks. "We'll have time for a real meal by the time we reach the log house."

He looked in Amy's direction and she quickly averted her gaze. He gave Brooke her drink without looking at her then walked over to Amy and handed her a bottle. "Are you okay?" Amy nodded without meeting his gaze. "We'll talk when we get to the lodge."

She nodded.

Between him and the ranch hands, they watered the animals at the little waterhole that graced the land during the rainy season. The small waterhole was how the ranch got its name.

Thirty minutes later, Nevada and the ranch hands rounded up the cattle and they set out for the last lap of their ride for the day. The sun had set over the horizon when they penned the cattle and rode into the lodge.

Amy came off the horse stiffly and Nevada wanted to beat himself for asking her to come along. "I'll help you with your horse." He took her reins.

She released it without protest. "I'm going to find Sam."

"Go on, I'll find you later." He would get this talk done tonight, no matter what.

· · ⌘ · ·

AMY FELT NEVADA'S PRESENCE before he walked into the dining hall. Her heart took up some calisthenics. Dressed in faded jeans and tee-shirt, he'd discarded his cowboy hat. His hair was still damp.

Nevada took his seat at the end of the table, leaving the chair at the head empty. Her father would've been there. Amy heaved a sigh. What if Dad didn't have capable hands? She knew next to nothing about what to do. The thought further endeared her to Nevada.

He gave a smile that included everyone. "I hope no one is exhausted?"

"A little tired but it's worth it, don't you think so sweetheart?" Mrs. Rudolph asked her husband.

"Yeah, it is my dear especially that you are here. I'm seeing everything through your eyes." He kissed her and Amy caught Nevada's gaze on her.

She stood quickly feeling the heat creep up her neck and making its way into her face. "Let me help Sam." She beat a hasty exit into the kitchen.

Sam gave her a puzzled look but didn't say anything. "Which one should I carry?"

"The big casserole bowls over there."

Amy made the trip to the dining room and as soon as she set her foot at the door, Nevada eased out of the chair taking it from her. Amy withdrew and Nevada caught up with her. "Your face betrays you."

"It's not funny. Why were you looking at me?"

"If you weren't looking at me, how would you know I was looking?"

She snorted and continued on to the kitchen. "I haven't seen your girlfriend. I guess she's primping all she can for you."

He let out a laugh and she elbowed him. "Are you jealous, Amy?"

"Me, jealous?"

"The lady doth protest too much, methinks."

She walked past him and entered the kitchen. Amy knew she was jealous so she offered no further comment. When she would've taken the next bowl and walked out, Nevada's hand snaked out and held her arm. He gave Sam a quick hug and kiss, "Thanks, Sam."

She glanced at him, then her gaze flickered between the two of them. "What have you done to get her so riled up?"

Amy tugged her hand from his but he held fast. All along the trail she'd told herself that whatever he did didn't bother her. Yet watching the two of them as they talked, she had realized it did bother her.

Initially, Angel's word had helped but after some time she wasn't sure. "Let go of my hand." She hated the quiver in her voice.

Nevada reached out and tilted her chin but she turned her head. "We will talk tonight, Amy. I'll find you."

He released her hand and Amy turned and walked through the back door.

Chapter Twenty-eight

Brooke came into the dining room. Just like her to walk in when all was set. There was the contrast between the two women. Brooke loved to be served, Amy served. She took the seat beside him and when her legs touched his, he moved slightly.

Amy hadn't returned. He hadn't planned to make her angry and there was no way he'd have talked to her in the presence of anyone else. That was why he had let her go. He only hoped that giving her opportunity to hold onto her dignity hadn't made him come off as nonchalant.

He looked towards the door. Maybe he should go and check on her. She walked in just then.

"I hope you haven't waited on account of me." she said, taking a seat beside Sam. She didn't look at him but at least he could see she'd gained her composure.

Nevada said the grace and bowls of foods were passed around. After the first course, he insisted Sam sit down and, between him and Amy, they took the dishes and replaced them with another. As they served others, Nevada thought again how Brooke would've been too much of a liability at the ranch.

She was comfortable sitting and eating while she was served. Amy wouldn't do that.

Sometimes, when things didn't work out, one would feel as if everything had gone wrong with life. Brooke only imagined she wanted him again. If she knew what came along with life on the ranch, she'd change her mind.

Amy ate quietly not attempting to join in the discussion.

Nevada didn't make any effort either. He'd have to do the talking as soon as he could. Only he couldn't help the fact that he had guests he was responsible for.

"I'll help wash up. You can all head out to the living room. I'll catch up with you." He caught up with Sam. "Please, go take your rest. We have a full day tomorrow."

"I just need—"

He shook his head. "Nothing more for tonight. Please."

Sam excused herself to her room. The woman was something else. Alone with Amy, maybe they could talk now.

"I'll help too," Brooke said, walking into the kitchen.

Amy looked at him and dropped the towel. "I wouldn't want to be in your way then." She stepped past him.

"Amy, I'll find you later."

She didn't respond. Silence hung in the air following her exit.

"What is wrong with her?"

"Brooke, don't even start. I don't care to discuss Amy with you. If you have anything else to say, fine, if not, keep your opinion and let's work."

She huffed and pouted, but kept quiet. A half hour later they finished the chores.

Nevada checked to make sure the animals had been fed. It was drizzling. There wouldn't be anything outdoors tonight. He went to his room and picked up the guitar he'd loaded in the wagon. He'd learned from one of the men that played in the subway he usually slept in. Who knew where the man was now?

He made his way back to the sitting room. They had a game of chess going on. Angel sat in a corner; a bible opened on his lap. The rain had started in earnest, but it was a gentle fall, nothing like the one from last week.

He sat and watched them play. Nevada surveyed the faces of his guests. Fatigue was setting in. The young man had his arm around his wife, others were grumbling about the rain trapping them indoors.

"You play guitar?" Greg asked.

"A little."

"Can you play some songs?"

"I could. Anything to help you all pass the night. Since you asked, do you have a song in mind?"

"Play *Great is Thy Faithfulness.*"

Nevada balanced the bass guitar on his thigh. He had every reason to be grateful. One time it looked as though all hope was lost and here he was doing what he wanted to do. The whole future looked brighter. His faith had also received a boost in the process.

He strummed the strings and then smiled at his audience. The young wife cuddled closer to her husband. Even Angel put his bible aside.

They all waited. Nevada closed his eyes. "For Your glory Lord," he whispered as he started to play.

When he strummed the last line, they clapped. One song after another, he played far into the night. When they all left for the night, he told Brooke he was going to talk to Amy and to make herself scarce. He felt bad having to be hard on her but she invited herself, she'd better entertain herself.

He owed Amy an explanation and that he'd do.

• • ☙ • •

THE RAINS HAD CEASED. Amy laid down listening to the music coming from the living room.

Coward.

Why had she not stayed in the kitchen? Her eyes burned. It was so pathetic that one thing she hadn't allowed in her twenty-six years had crept in behind her and floored her big time.

What would Brooke think?

Amy realized the music had stopped too. Had everyone gone to sleep? Nevada would come, as he said he would.

She turned on her back and stared at the ceiling of the log house. Brooke would keep him from coming.

A soft knock filtered through the door.

Amy sat up and listened but didn't answer.

The knock sounded again. Afraid he'd wake up others who probably had gone to bed; she padded to the door and opened it. "You didn't think I could be sleeping?"

"I'm sorry," he looked away briefly and then back. "I won't get a wink of sleep knowing you believe what I think you do. Besides I doubt if you'd sleep either."

Ignoring his perception, she opted for tact. "And what do you think I believe?"

"Can you step out for a bit? I won't keep you unnecessarily."

She hesitated. Did she want to know? Maybe not, but she'd listen and then walk away. Trusting her heart to someone was too scary. "Go ahead. I'll be there in a moment." He didn't move. "Seriously," she said. "I'll be right there."

Amy needed to bring her heartbeat under control and gather herself together. After a few minutes, she draped a shawl over her shoulders and stepped out.

The after-rains smell enveloped her as she walked onto the patio. The night was tranquil, the breeze cool. The trees swayed gently.

Nevada stood, tall and elegant, his back to her. His hair had grown to his shoulders. With all he'd been doing on the ranch lately, he probably didn't have time to bother about getting a haircut.

Amy stood a few feet away and waited. He turned toward her and surveyed her with appreciation in his eyes. "You look beautiful tonight, Amy."

Warmth flushed through her and she smiled at him. "Thank you."

"Come have a seat."

Amy took the few steps to reach the patio bench and slid onto it.

"Amy, I want to apologize for Brooke. I didn't know she was coming. I wouldn't ask you to put yourself out only to treat you this way."

"It doesn't matter," she said shrugging. She wouldn't make a big deal about it.

He sat beside her, took her hand threading his fingers through hers. The butterflies in her belly took flight. "It matters to me, Amy. I wanted you to enjoy this ride. How do you think I feel watching you ride alone while knowing you were doing it because I asked?"

She tugged her hand from his. He had a way of making it difficult for her to think.

"You knew her before me...."

"I haven't had any form of contact with her in a while. I'm telling you the truth from my heart, Amy."

"So, how did she know about the trip?" Amy asked before she could stop herself. This wasn't how to prove that it didn't matter.

"She wouldn't say. You remember the girl I told you I dated last year? That's her. Unfortunately, she met this rich guy after we started going out—I didn't know at the time. I guess she realized what she'd miss dating a ranch hand." Nevada stood up facing her, arms folded across his broad chest.

Amy saw the pain of what he was saying flit across his gaze. It cost him to tell her this. "It was the first time I felt a real connection or what I thought was a real connection with another human."

A branch fell from a tree a little distance away and Nevada turned to look. After a brief moment he returned his gaze to her. She held his gaze and waited. "Brooke started picking quarrels over everything. After a few days, she finally told me she wasn't interested in me that I...." he trailed off and stared into the night.

Amy felt his pain. She stood up and came to him, touching his arm lightly. His muscles bunched under her fingers but he didn't pull away." You don't have to tell me, I understand."

"Do you?" He asked, his eyes searching hers. They looked dark and sad, he shifted.

"I owe you an explanation and I know I should have done this long ago. That day she told me I was a loser and left. I despaired but held out hope that she'd return, but she didn't. I had several challenges afterwards and I came to believe her words to me. I don't have a right to Waterhole Ranch but at some point, it was my ticket to fulfill my dream."

He pushed a hand through his hair and came back and sat down. "I later found out the real reason she left me. I don't have any idea how she found out about the trip unless she's been keeping tabs on me somehow."

"I believe you. It was childish of me to behave the way I did." Amy took her seat again.

He stared at her for a long moment. "Amy you're not childish. I know you said you want to be friends and I'm sorry I've taken a few liberties... I want you to know today, Amy Jayden, I may not be the kind of man you want but Brooke is not the woman for me."

She inhaled the scent that was all Nevada and wanted to cry. Why would he say he wasn't the man for her? After all he told her today and all she'd seen, he was more than she wanted in a man.

"I've fallen in love with you, right from the day I set my eyes on you. I told myself that you're not for me but my head and heart won't listen. I'm not saying this to upset you but to clear the air between us. You have nothing to fear with Brooke."

Her heart swelled and crashed at the same time when she realized what he'd said. He loved her but he would never see himself as good enough...

"I've put both of you side by side and she's found wanting."

He smiled but a look of defeat crossed his eyes. "Thanks for listen-ing and believing me."

She couldn't swallow the lump that lodged in her throat. Too bad she wished she'd not set to course what had led to this.

He reached out and caressed her face briefly. "We have a long day tomorrow. I'll wait for you to get in," he said a small smile playing on his lips.

She took two steps to him, pulled his head down and kissed him lightly on the lips. Then, Amy turned without a backward glance and headed for her room.

Chapter Twenty-nine

He shouldn't read anything into the kiss. Sure, she wanted to make him feel better but it hadn't. It had stoked the longing in him, longing for a love between them that could never be.

The few times he kissed her she hadn't pulled away. That was twice if he included the one when she asked him to thank her. He wished he had something to offer Amy, then he'd be able to ask her to give them a chance.

Now he couldn't. He'd confessed his love for her but she hadn't said anything.

Nevada plowed a hand through his hair and let out a groan. He wouldn't get any sleep tonight and now that he had cleared the air, he'd better face reality.

He retired to his room and after wrestling with his thoughts for a while, he turned them to God. He didn't know when he succumbed to sleep.

. . ᢙᡒ . .

SAM RANG THE KITCHEN bell signaling everyone to the dining room. Amy walked in with a large bowl of grits which she placed beside bowls of country sausages and bacon. There was also hash browns and gravy, biscuits and buttery toast and syrups to go with them, whatever was to the choosing of everyone.

Nevada walked in after her and placed a towering plate of silverware on the table. He sat beside Amy.

His hand brushed hers and she met his gaze briefly and looked away. Awareness simmered between them. Things would never be the same now he'd told her how he felt. She wasn't looking down her nose at him like he was afraid she would.

No one noticed the exchange between them, oh, except Brooke who made it her duty to watch them. He chose to ignore her. Everyone settled down and fixed their plates. Nevada said the grace again.

"Everyone sleep well?" Sam asked as she checked to see that all was available that was needed.

"Slept like a baby," Greg said. "And I must say this is a meal fit for a king."

"Why, thank you. I had help," she said, a fond smile toward Amy.

When Amy first came home, Nevada had told himself he neither had time nor inclination for an attraction to her but all that had changed. With every thoughtful action she wormed deeper into his heart.

Across from him, Brooke sat giving him a baleful look. "You should ask me how my night was."

Nevada hiked up a brow. "Quit whining. I told you this wasn't some pleasure ride," he added softening his tone.

Matt grinned, "Man, that's no way to treat a fiancée. I haven't seen you take good care of her."

"Because we're not what she's making us out to be." He inclined his head giving her a coy smile. "Will you say otherwise?" He dared her to deny. He was glad to see her squirm. She'd set herself up. He took pity on her. "I hope your night was good."

She mumbled a response and Nevada turned to his meal. Others took his cue and dug into theirs. Meal completed, Nevada glanced at his watch and he stood up. "It's 8:00."

Lunch packs were passed around to be eaten somewhere on the trail. "Today, we'll split into our groups like yesterday. We have our outdoor camp five miles from here and the next set of pens another ten miles away. Angel and the others rode out early this morning to set camp, so they'll have it ready by the time we arrive."

He waited to be sure everyone was listening. "When we ride out now, we'll lead the cattle fifteen miles. Then we return to camp, meaning we have twenty-five miles ahead of us today. You all did well, like pros, yesterday, so you shouldn't have any problems. I'll make trips between the groups and attend to any problems you may have, just give me a holler.

"Watch out for snakes. On a cool day like this, they could lurk around. Last, but not least, stay on your horses. As long as you do that, you'll be fine. Any questions?"

They all shook their heads. "Great. I'd appreciate it if everyone would clear their dishes and give it a quick wash, that way we leave more time for Sam to do her cooking wonders," he said with a smile as he picked him up.

He winked at Amy when she walked past. He'd decided to leave all in God's hand and that meant living a normal life with Amy. And normal meant he wasn't going to bug her with his feelings. One time was enough; particularly since he couldn't do anything about it.

Nothing had changed; she was his boss and he? Just another ranch hand.

• • ❧ • •

AMY HAD MADE UP HER mind that she'd do the right thing. Brooke hadn't said anything to her good or bad. She didn't have to. Her hostility was palpable; Amy could have been one of Pharaoh's plagues. "Brooke, how are you doing?"

She snorted, "Like you care."

"I do. I have no complaint against you."

"I do."

Amy chose to ignore her cocky attitude. "The name is Amy Jayden."

"Yeah, daughter of the ranch owner. I made it my business to know who you are. With you around, Nevada will not give me any attention."

Amy could tell her she shouldn't look to someone else for the source of her problems. Her plan was to try and be friendly, but this wasn't getting her anywhere. "I hope we can be friends."

Her lips turned down and she gave Amy a once over. "Hope all you want. You are my competition and I do not plan on being friends with you."

Amy waited debating what else to do. Brooke turned and made to go. "Suit yourself, then."

Amy turned to her horse just as Nevada made an appearance. He looked between her and Brooke, then changed direction towards them. "Did she say something to you?"

"No, I just wanted to see if we could be friends. Don't take her to task. I was the one who approached her."

Nevada's gaze bore into hers and she held it steady. He gave her that lopsided smile that had a way of melting her heart. "You have a good heart Amy, but not everyone is like you."

She nodded. Her efforts had been rebuffed. She made to get on her horse.

"Hey, you need help?"

"No, thanks."

Angel signaled to him. He smiled at her and rode away.

Amy soaked in the peace and quiet of the early morning. The sun soothed her, making her feel drowsy. Disappointment threatened to color her enjoyment as Brooke came into view but she pushed it away.

She couldn't change who she was or what Nevada felt for her. She had yet to tell him he wasn't alone in his feelings. The time wasn't right. In singles and doubles, they rounded up the cattle and directed them to the pen where the veterinarian would look at them.

She looked up and saw Nevada ride from the other group towards theirs. He looked tall and in control. *Seest thou a man diligent in his works, he shall stand before kings and not mere men.*

Nevada was diligent, everything Sam had said about him Amy had observed for herself. Why would she not fall in love with him?

"Are you okay?"

"Yes."

"You were looking at me strangely." She flushed and lowered her head. Had she been staring? "You'd make a good cowgirl, you know?"

"I don't think so. I'm more an office girl."

"I bet you'd be good at whatever you set your heart to do, like you are doing now riding and rounding up cows."

"You're trying to make me feel good but I know if you leave me by myself, I wouldn't know a thing to do."

They took a wide berth around the animals to ensure that they went in the right direction.

"I doubt that you wouldn't know what to do. You might just need to hone the skills you knew before. Moreover, no one was born with ranching skills. The best of us learned and I'm not saying this to make you feel good."

She spared him a glance and he smiled at her. An animal veered off from the track and they had to abandon discussion to tackle it. After that, he rode away towards Mr. Rudolph who had signaled to him.

Would the time ever be right to tell him she loved him? Maybe she should've said so yesterday.

• • ❦ • •

"DO YOU THINK THE LEG is broken?" He looked around where the animal had taken a tumble. It must have been a rodent's hole that softened in the rain.

He leaned down feeling the joint above the fetlock. The leg wasn't broken, maybe sprained.

"Thank you, Mr. Rudolph. We'll get it taken care of. We have a short distance to go, after that you can do some of your bird watching," Nevada said smiling.

The young man rewarded him with a smile. "I plan to make a scrap-book from this ride. My wife has taken a lot of pictures and we hope to find some rare species here."

He tipped the brim of his hat toward Nevada and rode away. Nevada let the injured cow join in the trail at a slower pace to reach the pen.

The sun had already dipped behind the trees when they rode to the camp. They soon had a campfire going. By tomorrow, they'd head back to the ranch. He could say this first trip was a success.

Chapter Thirty

Two days later, Nevada sat in the den updating the ledger. The sound of a vehicle reached him. He frowned. It didn't sound like the truck Amy and Sam went out in.

Since he was the only one around, he decided to investigate. He got to the door and stopped.

Mr. Dylan's car sat beside the second ranch truck. Nevada wanted to turn back but Dylan had seen him.

The man's smile was tentative.

A much older man climbed out of the passenger side.

It definitely wasn't what he was thinking. Was it?

"Uh, hi." Dylan said, and then rushed on. "We'd like to see Ms. Jayden."

He lounged against the door jamb. Amy didn't go ahead with plans to sell, did she? "She isn't around. Have you tried her cell?"

"She isn't answering."

Nevada remembered he'd heard the phone ring earlier.

"Tell her to call me."

"What if we take a look around?" the man Dylan had chosen not to introduce asked.

"Why would you do that?" Nevada couldn't help asking.

"Oh, I'm John Huddleson, the buyer for the ranch."

Dylan hurried him away.

Nevada shook his head. How had he been so stupid? In his wildest imagination, he and Amy were on the same page.

The ranch truck turned into the driveway just then. He strode into the den, grabbed his Stetson, and walked out. Back in his room at the bunkhouse, he began throwing his stuff into the hold-all bag.

Pressure built in his chest until he saw stars. Nevada growled, kicked off the bag and watched it topple to the ground.

There was a tentative knock at the door which he chose to ignore.

He knew the moment Amy stepped in at the door. He hated the way his heart reacted to her presence and his defenses rose. "Do you know anything about privacy?" he said without turning.

"Nevada."

He turned and gave her a tight smile. "You finally got what you wanted." When she opened her mouth, he went on. "You don't have to justify yourself to me, Amy. I let my emotions run away and you played me for a fool."

"Will you just listen?"

He grabbed his carry-all and brushed past her.

"What happens to the ranch?"

"I'll be here until he takes over, for your father's sake." Nevada walked out. He wasn't sure where he'd spend the night: he just needed to be out of there.

He wanted to hear what she had to say, but a part of him knew this was what she'd always wanted. It wasn't even three months yet.

Her selling was not his problem. The fact that she led him on, when all the while she'd still kept contact with Dylan was really something. He didn't learn his lesson with Brooke, but Amy had driven his foolishness home.

Nevada walked past the ranch house and headed down the road. He shouldn't be feeling crushed, but with every step he took farther away from the ranch, the weight of her betrayal lay heavy on his shoulders.

• • ❧ • •

MEL ENTERED THE LIVING room and came to a stop. Amy could feel Mel's gaze on her but Amy kept her eyes trained on the city skyline.

"It's been two days since you came back. You want to tell me about the long face?"

"I'm jobless, burned all my bridges." She smiled amidst the pain that knifed at her heart. So much for trusting her heart to a man who would judge her without as much as a hearing.

"You were only contemplating coming on and off, right?"

"No. I rejected the offer." She sighed, the feeling that hung on her like a wet blanket pressing down on her shoulders.

"It's not the reason you're gloomy."

"Can we not talk about this?"

Mel sat beside her and held her hand. "Maybe you need to talk about it so you'll feel better. It's you and Nevada."

It was a statement. Amy used her thumb to wipe the tears that came. She nodded.

"Oh, come on." Mel pulled her into a hug.

"I wasn't planning to sell anymore."

Mel put her away, holding her by the shoulders. "What are you saying? It's about the ranch, right?"

Amy nodded.

"Calm down and tell me what happened."

She swallowed. "I had a property agent come check the ranch at the beginning. I wasn't sure what the outcome of my agreement with Nevada would be, so I told him to keep looking for a buyer."

She wiped her eyes. "I totally forgot to tell him to stop when things started looking up. Dylan showed up two days ago with a buyer. They'd apparently talked with Nevada."

"Didn't you try to explain to him?"

"He didn't want to hear anything. He still believes it's what I wanted."

"Did you try again after that?"

She shrugged. "He doesn't live on the ranch anymore, and he's refused to answer his phone."

Mel hugged her again. "I'm so sorry." After a moment, Mel set her away. "What do you plan to do?"

"I came to pack the rest of my stuff. I'll go home, figure out how to run the ranch and go from there."

"That means you won't sell anymore."

"No." She wiped her eyes. "I'll make the ranch work even if I die trying."

"Then, maybe you can convince Nevada that both of you are on the same page."

"He makes himself scarce—"

"You, my friend, are a smart woman. I'm sure you'll find him if you really want to."

Amy locked gazes with Mel. It was true. The last couple of days had been an eye opener for her. She wasn't sure she could convince Nevada but she'd give it a shot. If she failed at least she'd know she tried.

• • ✤ • •

"IT'S BEEN TWO WEEKS, Nevada. If Amy's planning to sell like you think, where is this buyer?" Angel asked.

Nevada shrugged, broke off a part of the stick he held in his hand and threw it in front of him. "She's gone back to her life. I can imagine she's just waiting for the three-month mark," he said bitterly.

It was too dark now to see. They had longer days with dark not falling until almost nine. But that was two hours ago.

He avoided going to bed until late these days to keep from tossing and turning.

Sam had been on his case to get himself back to the ranch. He should've been grateful Amy wasn't around, except that the ranch felt empty without her and he missed her acutely.

"You've been looking as though your world has come crumbling down."

"You're beginning to sound like Sam."

"In the mouths of two witnesses." Angel chuckled.

"Is it that obvious?"

"You're not much of a talker, I get that, but, these days, you hardly say a word, just work from dawn to dusk." Angel slapped him on the shoulder. "Have you looked in the mirror lately?"

"Don't even go there."

"Maybe I should. But, seriously, call Amy."

"And say what?" Nevada spread his hands.

"You didn't listen to her before. Maybe you should just call to say you're checking on her." Angel shrugged. "It's just in the off chance that she'd want to talk about it."

"That's a long shot. I don't know if she would want to speak to me now." His face warmed. "I ignored her calls the first two days and she stopped calling."

"More reason to be the one to make the move now."

Nevada scratched his two-week-old beard. There was still the possibility she planned to sell. What happens then?

He wasn't going to call. No point starting what had no future. They would just be right where they were now. He only hoped she found happiness where she was.

Angel stood and clapped Nevada on the shoulder. "Don't think too much about it, do it."

Nevada nodded. But he didn't plan to follow through. Not because he didn't want to, but as far as he knew, nothing had changed.

. . ❧ . .

AMY SLIPPED HER FEET out of her pumps. Her bags sat beside her in the kitchen. She was home for good. And it felt right.

Sam was all smiles as she handed Amy a glass of water. "You're just too full of surprises these days. You could at least warn me you were coming."

"I'm sorry, Sam. I didn't want anybody knowing in the off chance that Nevada would hear and disappear."

Sam sighed. "That one has become a recluse. Even I hardly see him."

"Do you happen to know where he'd be now?"

Sam searched her face. "He took the horse and rode out. I assume it's where he always goes."

"I know the place. I'm just going to change now and then I'll go find him."

"I think he misses you, even though he won't say."

The butterflies in Amy's stomach fluttered. Dared she hope?

Sam looked through the window. "We still have a few hours of daylight. But don't stay out too late."

"I won't." Amy kissed her cheek and ran up to her room to change.

"By the way I love your hair," Sam shouted after her.

"Thanks." Amy's heart beat in anticipation. She glanced at her reflection in the hallway mirror. Her red hair had been cut short and styled to form ringlets around her face. Mel said she looked like a baby angel with a halo. Amy only hoped the do over Mel forced her into was worth it.

By the time she came down, doubt was assailing her.

"You don't want to miss him. Get going."

Amy bit her lip and then stepped out of the kitchen. By the time Amy reached the creek, she was covered in a fine sheen of sweat.

Nevada squatted beside the creek, his back to her, but he must've heard the sound of her horse.

He turned.

His eyes lit and swiftly dimmed in split seconds. He stood slowly like he was trying to decide whether he was seeing her for real.

Amy slid down from the horse.

For minutes, they stared at each other, Amy's heart pounding until she feared she'd suffer a cardiac arrest. "I'm back." Her voice wobbled a little.

He nodded, pushing his hands deep in his pockets. Nevada didn't keep this much beard. Was that an indication that he felt her absence like she did his?

"You had a good trip?"

"Yes."

He nodded again. A moment of awkward silence followed.

"What are you doing out here?"

Amy bit her lip. "I came to see you. Look," she rushed on, "I want you to know how sorry I am about Dylan. I had totally forgotten about him. He wasn't supposed to show up at all."

She twisted the reins in her hand and then let them go.

A myriad of emotions flickered across his gaze, each quickly disappearing and replaced by another—surprise, caution, hope...

"What are you saying, Amy?"

She swallowed. "I'm saying I was never planning to sell, haven't thought of that in weeks. You made me fall in love with you and the land."

He walked towards her, stopping a few feet away.

"There was no way I'd make all your efforts feel like a waste, after all you've done."

He searched her face.

What was going on in his mind?

"Why would I quit my job and still sell the ranch?"

He looked away and plowed a hand through his hair.

Amy closed the gap. "Nevada, I can't go back to what I was because you have made me find a *new* me. Don't you see that?"

He faced her. "I thought it was what you always wanted..." She shook her head. "I should have listened to you. Can you forgive me?"

"I wanted to sell at first, wanted it with every breath. It was like shedding the old skin. But, not anymore. I love you, Nevada Logan. I hope I'm not too late."

Nevada smiled. "Does that mean you've forgiven me?"

"Maybe."

He chuckled. "What would you want me to do? Ask away. I'll go to the moon and back if that's what you want."

"Shut up and kiss me."

"That's pretty easy." He looked her over. "Your hair." He touched the ringlet that fell over her forehead.

"You like it?" She smiled tentatively, her face warming. "I did it for you."

Nevada stroked her cheek with the back of his hand. "I love it. I love you too, Amy Jayden, and you look amazing."

He pulled Amy closer. The wild beating of his heart echoed hers against her palm that lay against his chest.

"Amy," he started and stopped.

Amy waited. If she had to hold on forever to hear what he had to say, she'd gladly do so. "I'm all ears."

"I don't want to stop working for you."

"That's fine."

"And you won't mind dating this employee of yours?"

"Is that a request to go out with you?"

He closed his eyes, a smile on his lips. "Not a cute one, right? I want us to explore us, see how we go from there. What do you say?"

"Yes."

"Yes, you'll go out with me or yes, it's not a cute request?"

She giggled. "Both."

He brushed his lips against hers. "Thank you."

"For?"

"Making me a happy man."

"No, I should be the one thanking you for saving me."

She pulled his head down and kissed him.

Epilogue

Amy slipped her feet into the cowboy boots. She rose and the huge skirt of her wedding gown pooled around her. She looked through the window of her room across the white snow-covered grounds to the barn that had been transformed into a winter wonderland.

Red and green garland proclaimed, along with the white fairy lights, that this was a double celebration—Christmas and her wedding day.

"You look beautiful, girlfriend. I'm green with envy," Mel said, wiping her eyes.

"I see the way Angel looks at you and I'm wondering..."

"What?" Her blush said she noticed it too.

"My new foreman has a thing for you."

Mel ducked and picked up the handmade tiara fashioned like a cute little Stetson and set it on Amy's curls. "I don't know what you're talking about."

"How are the tables suddenly turned? Months ago, you were the one telling me about Nevada. Time flies, huh?"

It'd been six months since Nevada asked that they explore their relationship. Six months of bliss. Yeah, they still had their moments but she had no doubt in her heart that Nevada loved her.

The door opened. Sam bustled in. Her face, pink from the cold, was wreathed in a smile. "You look amazing, love. Your mom and dad would be proud of you."

"Thank you." Her voice wobbled. She wished her parents were here. Angel's dad had agreed to give her away.

Sam clucked her tongue. "Now don't go ruining your makeup. Go meet that young man. And you better treat him well, or you'll have me to deal with."

Amy laughed. She knew she was bound to give Nevada more trouble than he'd give her with her love for talking...

"Let's go." Mel held the long train of her gown.

Mel opened the door. Frigid wind blasted Amy's face, stealing her breath for a moment. As she stepped out of the ranch house and walked towards the huge barn, she couldn't help but thank God for how He'd changed her life in the past year. She remembered her losses, every day, but in all of it she'd been comforted.

She stepped into the barn as the wedding march began. Nevada stood in front of the makeshift altar, all cowboy to the boots, his smile as wide as the bright sky that marked their day. This was one of the best decisions she'd made in her life—marrying Nevada.

"You're beautiful," he mouthed.

"You look good too."

She turned and handed over her bouquet to Mel. Her face was bright red. Amy located the source—her foreman and the best man.

Her lips turned up.

Nothing could be better than both of them finding love.

She turned to Nevada and smiled.

Sneak Peek: LOVING ROYALTY

Chapter One

The cool evening breeze of Blue Song sent the tree branches waving merrily in its caress, a contrast from the gloom that threatened to rip her heart straight out of her chest.

Jordan slid to her haunches, her back against the wall in the living room. She wrapped her arms around her body in a bid to ease the shaking.

Luke paced a few feet from her. He didn't get it. Did he?

"I don't understand. Is this a ploy to break up with me or you really don't remember me, Jay?"

"You think this is my idea of a joke?"

"You tell me." He pointed to his chest, his eyes blazing with anger. "How come you remember your family and not me?"

"I. Don't. Know!" She covered her face for a moment. "Maybe I need more time."

"How long?" he asked in barely controlled voice.

"I don't know."

"This is what frustrates me about the whole thing, Jordan. How long are we talking about here? And don't say you don't know anymore."

He must be really upset now. In the past months, he'd called her Jay. "You think I like being this way? You have supported me for the past six months plus and I'm grateful. But, to tell you the truth, I don't know me. I don't know a lot of things. I'm feeling my way through life. Can't you understand that?"

He just stood there staring at her. Really, why did she not remember him? Her doctor said she shouldn't push things but she was tired of not knowing. They didn't have the answers she so desperately needed.

Salty tears slipped into her mouth and she swiped it off angrily. She hated being vulnerable, weak, so out of control. "The doctor said I have selective memory loss. No one understands why I remember some things and not others."

He plowed a hand through his hair. "I know what the doctor said."

His shoulders slumped. Jordan searched his face. Was he relenting? At this point, she wasn't sure what she wanted. A part of her wanted him to hold her, tell her he would stick through this period with her, but the other part couldn't connect with him.

"I wish I knew what we're dealing with here—a month, two, three. But, six months, going on seven and nothing?"

He squatted before her and took her hands. "Tell me, who am I to you? Just a random guy hanging around and hoping for what? That my girlfriend will wake up one day and figure out who I am."

Jordan ignored the tears tracking down her face. "I don't..." He didn't want to hear that, so she said instead, "I'm sorry."

"I'm sorry, too." He rose. "I hate...to do this, but," his voice caught. "I just can't keep on like this. I can't be with someone who doesn't know me."

All she could do was nod. He stooped down and kissed her on the head. He turned away but not before she glimpsed the tears in his eyes.

She'd hurt him.

He headed for the door. Jordan wanted to call him back, but what would she say? She was tired of the long wait that one day she would remember spontaneously what her life was before now. That seemed like a pipe dream.

The door shut softly behind him. With finality. She dropped her head into her hand to ease the pounding that was starting up.

Ever since she woke up on that hospital bed and realized she'd lost her memory, she did her best not to get emotional. But this was too much. Sobs wracked her body. She'd lost one more person in her ever-shrinking circle.

The sound of a vehicle and slamming of doors penetrated her mind, but Jordan couldn't make herself move.

Footsteps sounded closer. Jordan stood up from the floor and wiped her eyes. Within seconds, Dana turned the corner.

"We saw Luke leaving." She looked at Jordan. "What happened? You two got into a fight?"

She draped her arm around Jordan and led her to the sofa. Jordan leaned against the backrest. Her head was pulsating along with her heartbeat. As much as she wanted to cry again, she held it at bay. "He broke up with me."

Jordan's older brother, Jesse walked in just then. He sat on the other side of her. "Luke told me. If he's quitting on you now, he doesn't deserve you."

She shook her head. Jordan glanced between her brother and friend. She didn't remember Dana and she hadn't had the heart to tell her so, especially when she saw pictures of both of them together. What they had now was a new friendship forged by Dana's persistence. Was that what she and Luke lacked? "It's not his fault. Why can I not remember him?"

Jesse took her hand. "I don't know."

Jordan closed her eyes and leaned back. What was the point of her life anyway? Dana scooted closer and wrapped Jordan in her arms. "I'm so sorry," she whispered.

She'd heard those words a million times over. She only wished those three words would right her world again.

Buy Loving Royalty here![1]

---

1. https://www.amazon.ca/Loving-Royalty-Cowboys-BlueSong-Book-ebook/dp/
B0833LN48F

GET FREE BOOKS AND EXCLUSIVE ROSE VERDE MATE-RIAL

Building a relationship with my readers is the best thing about writing. I send a weekly newsletter with details on new releases, special offers and other news tidbits relating to my writing.

And if you sign up to my mailing list I'll send you these for free"

1. A copy of In Plain Sight.
2. A novelette retelling of the book of Ruth.
3. A free copy of my novella, Christmas Wish

You can get the novel, novella and novelette, for free, by signing up at here[2]![3]

---

2. http://bit.ly/2K6GNdy

3. http://bit.ly/2K6GNdy

Enjoy this book? You can make a difference

Reviews are the most powerful tool in getting attention to my books. I wish I have the financial wherewithal to put up ads for them. But I don't. So I count on my amazing readers. Your honest reviews will help point others to my books. If you have enjoyed this book I would be grateful if you could spend a few minutes leaving a review, as short or as long as you like on the book's amazon page right here![4]

Thank you very much!

4.   https://www.amazon.com/Saving-Jayden-Cowboys-BlueSong-Book-ebook/dp/ B081K9C6Y7

ABOUT THE AUTHOR

Rose Verde is the author of Finding Love Medical Romance, The Cowboys of BlueSong and A Love Through Time series. She makes her online home right here![5] You can connect with Rose on Twitter[6], on FaceBook[7], and you can send an email at <u>email</u> if that feels like something you'd want to do.

---

5. http://roseverde.com

6. http://twitter.com/roseverde2016

7. http://fb.me/roseverde2020

ALSO BY ROSE VERDE
Have you read them all?
In Finding Love Medical Series
WHISPERS OF LOVE

Jordyn Rivers has her work cut out for her with her new client. She also has to deal with her client's brother who proves a bigger hurdle to overcome. Ty Warren thinks his sister's nurse is incompetent and he makes that very clear. But as he watches her tenderness with his sister, he realizes there's more to nursing than timetables, and maybe his jaded past is to be blamed for his reaction. His efforts change to aiding Jordyn. As they work together, and through their past, can he convince her to overcome her pain and fear, and give them a chance?

A CHANCE FOR LOVE

As an orphan, Kierra Nash is destined for life on the streets. A Christian agency provides her a second chance, getting her employment in the royal household of Prince Charles St. Vita. Her duty: take care of the spoiled eight-year-old, Princess Elsa who has already run off several nannies with her antics.

Prince Charles has never had anyone challenge his parenting skills, except the new nanny. And he's ready to listen. As Kierra and Charles work together to help Elsa, an attraction grows between them. But can a prince and a street girl bridge their differences?

DESTINED IN LOVE

When bad boy Chase Calder returns to town to fill-in for another doctor, Ruby Campbell knows there will be trouble. Their last disastrous encounter reminds her to keep their relationship strictly professional.

Chase is second guessing his return to a town where people's sins are never forgotten. And he has a fair share of those. To move on, he has to face his past sooner or later. He's also determined to win the one person he's hurt the most.

Ruby realizes as she works with Chase that he's changed. Can he convince her to trust him again and give them a second chance?

HOME FOR LOVE

After the death of her husband, Allison Myers returns to her hometown for a fresh start. Estranged from her parents, and medical bills piled high, she struggles to take care of her two young children.

Dr. Jared Reid is intrigued by the young nurse who works on his shift. When he finds out the devastation she's suffered, he offers her and her children the use of his remodeled basement. As the situation forces the two of them together, Jared finds it harder and harder to step away from the woman and two sweet children that have captured his heart. And the longer Allison depends on Jared, the more it will hurt when she has to leave.

If only she didn't have to leave.

SECOND SHOT AT LOVE

Stormie Johnson's neighbor continues to steal her designated parking spot, and she has to fix that once and for all. Except their discussion escalates into an argument. Not one to be confrontational, she chooses to ignore him. Until they meet again. In her classroom.

Dr. Jordan Price, a widower in a new city, has only two things on his mind—run a great ER team and care for his son. The attraction he has for his son's new teacher is the last thing he needs. Can they set aside all those reasons for a Second Shot At Love?

In A Love Through Time Series

A TIME TO HEAL

Having dropped out of college to care for her sick mom before she passed years ago, Raven Jamison only has two things on her plan: go back to school and get her life finally together. Until then, she throws herself into volunteering at the Great Smoky Mountain.

After being medically discharged from the US Marine, Landon Kendall is faced with uncertainties on every side. When he gets invited to spend Thanksgiving at his friend's, he reluctantly agrees. The spark between him and Raven can't be denied and they fight their growing attraction to each other. But the dark cloud that hangs over Landon's future proves there is no room for someone as fiery, fun-loving, and beautiful as Raven.

A TIME TO LAUGH

After breaking up with her boyfriend, along with the rollercoaster of emotion at home, Izzy needs time away. Not knowing what the future holds, she takes a trip to North Pole, Alaska to spend the holidays.

Luke finally gets promoted to the coveted position of hotel manager. But, he's faced with the reality that the demands of his job will take him away from his little girl. Finding a nanny in the middle of the Christmas season would be no walk in the park. He enlists the help of his aunt who owns a local inn.

That's where he meets Izzy, an out of towner who seems to be taken with his daughter. Except that Izzy is on vacation not babysitting duties. Convincing herself that it's only temporary, she agrees to watch the young girl. When sparks fly, Izzy wonders if she's made a wrong decision in agreeing. The secret she is hiding is bound to tear them apart.

A TIME TO LOVE

When Autumn Bryson's meddling aunt signs her up for a honeymoon cruise, Autumn concludes that her aunt has just upped the ante in her numerous schemes to marry Autumn off. Or, just maybe husbands fell from heaven these days. Until her mother's illness takes a turn for the worst and her dying wish is to see her daughter married. But to go on a honeymoon cruise requires being recently married ... and that Autumn is not.

Preston is focused on his job and caring for his child. When his boss proposes to him, he's hesitant to agree. Sure, he likes her, a lot. But – marriage? Except that what starts as an arrangement becomes love unexpected and a family for both of them.

A TIME TO DANCE

Wedding planner, Kathy Murray snags a high-profile client for a spring wedding at her family inn. A dream come true. But then, her brother insists their friend, her teenage crush, brings his expertise into play. Kathy plans to keep her heart on a leash and do her job.

For Mike Pierce, helping his friend pull off a wedding and bring some much-needed publicity to the family inn is his way of paying back years of friendship. Kathy doesn't seem to want him around for reasons he cannot fathom. But he's determined to win her trust and heart in the process.

Is the wedding weekend enough to undo whatever mistrust she has for him? Is it enough time for Kathy to let go and let love?

In Cowboys of BlueSong Series

SAVING AMY JAYDEN

After the news of her father's accident, Amy Jayden returns to the ranch and the memories she'd abandoned long ago. Hoping to be in and out quickly, her plans are crushed when her father doesn't make it. With a heavy heart, and a soul riddled with guilt, she has to decide what to do with the ranch her father left to her.

Nevada Logan, foreman of the Water Hole Ranch, is broken to find out his boss and close friend is gone. He has no trust in the daughter who would rather sell than hold on to her father's legacy. The two find themselves bumping heads at every turn. That is ... until love finds its way into each of their hearts.

LOVING ROYALTY

An accident leaves Jordan Holt with amnesia. Her boyfriend can't take being forgotten and breaks up with her. She begins creating new memories, including riding competitions—another lost memory. Love is the last thing on her mind. Until Eric.

Prince Eric Arthur Phillips escapes the humiliation of being left at the altar by fleeing to rural Ontario. It was supposed to be for a few days. Until a certain horse jumper grabs his heart. She thinks he's another employee of theirs, not royalty. And he's missed opportunities to tell the truth.

Can their budding relationship survive when she finds out the secret he's keeping?

LASSOED BY LOVE

Magazine journalist Chrystolle Spencer has to refuse her cousin's request for her to house-watch. Her slave-driver boss will never let her take the time off. Until he gives her an ultimatum—write a jaw dropping article for the magazine or pack her bags. Maybe she can do both.

Wyatt Danner hasn't been on a bull since the accident that almost left him crippled. He refuses to give up on his dream and has worked hard to get back on the circuit. When he agrees to feed his neighbor's animals while they are away, he's surprised to find Crissy staying in their home. From their first meeting, Wyatt and Crissy clash in every way possible.

The feelings between them can't be denied, but are there too many complications to make it work?

DEDICATION

I'd like to first thank God for giving me the gift of storytelling. Without Him, I can do nothing. Thank you to my family who encourage me and my kids who are proud of their author mom. Also, a special thanks to my Patricia Bell and a couple other great friends who read this book and gave their opinion. Your advice and critiques are greatly appreciated. To my editor, Lisa Bartholomew, thanks!

www.ingramcontent.com/pod-product-compliance
Lightning Source LLC
Chambersburg PA
CBHW031125130726
47988CB00006B/2224